ACCIDENTAL SUPERSTAR

MARIANNE LEVY

First published 2016 by Macmillan Children's Books

This revised edition published 2017 by Macmillan Children's Books
an imprint of Pan Macmillan
20 New Wharf Road, London N1 9RR
Associated companies throughout the world
www.panmacmillan.com

ISBN 978-1-5098-6581-9

For Willow

The picture quality's not the best. But even so, it's clear I'm having a good time. I'm smiling so much you can see all my teeth, and I'm shutting my eyes on the high notes and everything. And my voice sounds all right, I think. Not perfect, but not terrible, either.

It's a shame you can also see a pack of extra-strong blackhead-removal cream on my desk. And heaps of clothes on my bedroom floor. And something round and fluffy sticking out from under the bed that I think was once a pepperoni pizza.

If I'd known that two million people were going to be watching, I'd probably have done a bit of tidying up.

CHAPTER ONE

'Amanda, will you please turn it down? Some of us are trying to work.'

Basically, my sister had got her first pay cheque and bought a new stereo, which she had on pretty much 24/7. Even at night. Especially at night.

Meanwhile Lacey had cut her own fringe and because it didn't look completely terrible was putting serious pressure on me to join her. Honestly. You get whole entire lessons on how to deal with people offering you cigarettes and drugs, but no one prepares you for your best friend clicking a pair of scissors in your face and saying, 'It'll really show off your eyes.'

Oh, and Mum and Dad's divorce had come through. So there was that.

Otherwise it was a normal sort of a Saturday morning and I was lying on my bed supposedly doing my English but in fact doodling lyrics, because that's how I like to warm up for homework. Of course, sometimes I spend so long on the warm-up I run out of time before I reach the main event.

The problem is that writing songs is just so much more interesting than homework. Writing songs is more interesting than anything. Except listening to songs that other people have written, which is the *other* way I warm up for homework.

It is possible that I don't spend as much time on my homework as I should.

But this song wouldn't leave me alone. And for a second, I had it, there, whole in my head.

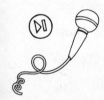
Gonna break out my make-up
For this stupid break-up

Then the pause, and then . . .

Thump thump, thump-thump thump.

'Amanda, will you turn it down, just for a second? I am in the middle of academic study.'

For just a second, the bass boom did stop. Then it started again.

'MANDA! My walls are VIBRATING.'

'You said just for a second!'

I grabbed my lyric book and wrote everything down

before it got away from me again, then pulled my guitar across the bed to get the tune into my fingers.

At which point the door opened.

'Katie, I thought you were doing homework?'

My big sister stood in the doorway and gave me one of her looks.

Amanda is tall, with a long face and a long nose and long fingers. But even though all the sticky-outy bits of her are thin, the middle bits are pretty solid. By which I mean, she's got broad shoulders and big hips and they make her look fatter than she is. I'm allowed to say that because I have them too. Then there's the Cox hair, which is mad, half curly, half straight, and the Cox skin, which is pale with an oily T-zone.

'I am about to start a very important essay on *Julius Caesar*, actually.'

Up went her eyebrows. 'And you're writing it on the guitar?'

'If only.'

Which Mands took as a signal to sit down on my bed, giving Shakespeare a close-up view of her bum. Which seemed as good a moment as any to call it a day.

It's like I always say with homework: you can push it

too far. It's really important to know when to stop.

'I liked what you were playing just now,' said Amanda.

I played it again.

'Does it have words?'

I had a go at singing it. Only, it didn't come out fun and defiant like I'd intended it to. It just came out a bit sad.

'Do you think,' said Amanda, 'that maybe you've written enough songs about the divorce?'

'What do you mean?'

'It's over and we're OK. So stop dwelling.'

For the record, there hadn't been *that* many. Which I told her.

'"Four-Fingered Twix" wasn't about the divorce! And "Home Sweet Home" wasn't either. Well, maybe a tiny bit.'

'*Goodbye bedroom*,' sang Amanda. '*Goodbye past. Homes like ours aren't made to last.* I'd say that was about the divorce. Wouldn't you?'

She had a point. But saying goodbye to the literal home of my entire childhood, how could I *not* write about it? All the good memories, like the guinea-pig babies and Easter-egg hunting and next-door's cat falling in the paddling pool, were in that house, and when Dad left we had to sell it. He used his half of the proceeds to rent a place in California where you can sometimes see dolphins from the kitchen window. We used our half to rent a flat in Harltree, a nowheresville just outside London, where what you can see from the kitchen window are foxes going through the bins.

In the end, divorce affects everything. Even the wildlife.

'You're bringing us down,' said my sister.

'Oh, blame it all on me. The big bad apple on the family tree.'

She laughed. 'You should put that in a song. Anyway, things change; people move on.'

'Dad certainly seems to have.'

'THIS IS WHAT I'M TALKING ABOUT.'

'I'm supposed to be miserable! I'm a teenager now. That's just me!'

'Doesn't sound like the Katie I know,' said Amanda, which was kind of her, given that it did sound like the Katie I knew, for the last few months, at least.

'You know what? You're right,' I said. 'From now on I will be *upbeat*.' I waved at the window, and any potential bin foxes, and plucked out a bit of a tune.

'*So* much better,' said Amanda. 'And anyway, it's not all doom and gloom. Mum's got a boyfriend.'

My fingers froze. 'What? No she hasn't.'

'She has.'

'Amanda, Mum isn't seeing anyone. She knows it's way too soon for that. I've told her.'

'Which is why she hasn't told you.'

'And she told *you*?'

Mands looked away. 'Not specifically. But there are signs.'

The thing about Amanda is that she's read too many fairy stories about happy ever afters and handsome princes and things. What she doesn't realize is that we had the perfect family. We were the perfect family. And then we weren't. And we never would be ever again.

No biggie.

'What signs?' I said.

'OK . . .' She ticked them off on her fingers. 'She's been singing in the shower.'

'Practising for karaoke.'

'She bought a new jacket.'

'It's been cold!'

'She's got –' Amanda paused for effect – 'the glow.'

'She went on a sunbed!'

'And why do you think that is?' said Amanda.

'I told you,' I said. 'It's been really cold. Can you please get your behind off my books?'

'OK, but listen—'

'No,' I said. '*You* listen. Mum was really messed up by all the Dad stuff. It took her ages to get even slightly sorted and she's only just got herself into anything like an OK place. I hardly think she'd go and mess that up with someone new right now.'

Amanda stood up. 'Not with you telling her she can't – *Urgh!* What's that?'

I had a look. 'Pizza.'

'Katie, we had pizza three nights ago. You are revolting.'

'Then you are free to amuse yourself elsewhere.'

So she got up and left.

After that I did *try* to do my homework. I tried to write a new song too, because that tune I'd come up with was properly catchy. I played it over and over and over again, only, instead of lyrics, all I could think about was Mum.

Which is when I heard her key in the door.

 9

'Katie? Are you home? I feel like I haven't talked to you properly in ages!'

'I'm in my room,' I said.

'Coming!'

There was no way she was glowing, although it was true that Mum did look a bit happier than she had been. Probably just the effect of her new jacket. And the haircut. And, was that an actual manicure . . . ?

'So,' I said. 'How're things? It's all been quite tough lately, hasn't it?'

'I suppose so,' said Mum.

'What with the move,' I said. 'And this place being so cramped.'

'It's growing on me,' said Mum.

'Like fungus,' I said.

I suppose I should describe our flat, but there's not much point. It had somebody else's curtains on the windows and someone else's hairy old carpet on the floor. So it wasn't really ours at all.

Mum was still going. 'I know things have been . . . well . . . But I feel like we're really turning a corner.'

'"We" as in . . .'

'Me, you, Amanda. Us.'

Which made me feel a little better. 'Maybe.'

'Definitely,' said Mum. 'It's like there's been a dark cloud over us, but you know what, summer's on its way, we're settled here now . . . we've made it, Katie.'

'Are you sure?' I said.

'I really do think we're going to be all right,' said Mum. 'So cheer up. Promise?'

I wasn't going to promise, but I did say, 'I'll try,' which was pretty much the same thing. Because maybe we would be all right, now. Mands was fairly annoying and I wasn't at all sure about Mum's taste in jackets but, all things considered – and there were a lot of things to consider – we'd made it through quite well.

'Are you all right to do dinner without me tonight? It's karaoke at the Dog and Duck.'

Mum is a complete karaoke fiend. I think her version of 'My Way' is better than the original. And the Elvis version. It's maybe up there with Nina Simone's.

'Is that why you're in such a good mood?' I said.

She flushed. 'They're a nice bunch in there. They don't ask about your father. And they like my singing.'

Of course they liked Mum's singing. How could they not?

 11

'So *that's* why you're so happy,' I said. 'It's funny, because Amanda thought you had a new boyfriend!'

There was this pause.

And then Mum said, 'Clever Amanda.'

'What? Why? Amanda isn't clever. Amanda doesn't know anything. You don't have a boyfriend.'

'He's called Adrian,' said Mum. 'I'm sure you'll like him a lot.'

I wanted to say: *Adrian? How long has this been going on for? And did you not think to maybe ask me first?*

'Adrian?' I said. 'How long has this been going on for? And, excuse me, but did you not think to maybe ask me first?'

'Only a couple of months,' said Mum. 'And I don't need your permission, Katie.'

'But I thought . . .' And then I ran out of words and just stared at her.

'He saw me singing a few times and said I had a nice voice, and then one thing led to another and . . .' I had to tune out for a bit. I came back in on, 'I'd never have started seeing him if I hadn't thought you could deal with it. He's lovely, Katie. I promise.'

'If he ever hurts you, I'll kill him with my bare hands.

And my straighteners, which are pretty lethal when they're heated up.'

She laughed, which was annoying, because I meant it.

'I'll have him over for lunch on Sunday. I'm sure you'll get on like a house on fire.'

At which point she went back downstairs. And I *did* feel like a house on fire.

Which I don't think was what Mum meant at all.

CHAPTER TWO

'I'm a bad person,' I said.

Lacey and I were walking along the canal to school. Which sounds all pretty and lovely and like it's full of boats and ducklings, but in fact is quite a risky way of getting somewhere, what with all the year seven boys and the incredibly dirty water.

'How do you mean, you're a bad person?' said Lacey.

'You're supposed to say, "No you're not",' I told her.

'OK, no you're not. Why?'

'Because Mum's found a new boyfriend and she's really happy and I know I should be happy too, but I'm not.'

'That's not so bad,' said Lacey.

'But you think it's a bit bad?'

'A bit,' said Lacey, and I decided I wouldn't be asking her for any more advice for the time being.

We stopped for a second to watch one of the boys trying to climb into a wheelie-bin.

'Did you know that Savannah's having a party?' said Lacey.

'Nope,' I said, still watching the boys in the bin.

'It's not for ages and ages but she's already got this exclusive guest list,' Lacey went on.

'You're making Savannah sound like some Hollywood A-lister,' I said.

'She *is* a Harltree A-lister,' said Lacey. 'Which makes us Harltree D-listers, I suppose.'

'Stop it, Lacey; you're overwhelming me with joy.'

'Maybe we're C-listers?' said Lacey.

'Nah, we're definitely D-list. If that.'

'Well, she can't just have the A-list at the party or there'll only be three of them there.'

That sounded like my last party. Me, Lacey and Mands, dancing to my collection of vintage *NOW* albums. 'That's OK,' I said. 'As long as it's the right three people.'

'Yes, but her dad's spending loads of money on it. There's going to be a tent in her garden. A really enormous one, with caterers and a light-up dance floor and everything.'

'Do you really reckon she'll invite the likes of us?' I said, thinking that maybe, if she did, I might get a shot at standing somewhere in the vicinity of Dominic Preston, who is incredibly good-looking.

Lacey looked a bit offended. 'She's invited me. Maybe it's my fringe. I think my hair is B-list, even if I'm not. You really need to consider cutting one in, Katie; it would completely open out your face.'

'I am considering it,' I said.

'I could do it tonight,' said Lacey hopefully. 'If you've got some sharp scissors.'

I made a mental note to text Mands and get her to hide the scissors.

'I think Adrian's going to be there tonight,' I said. 'Maybe we could go to yours.'

'Is he that bad?'

'I did try to like him,' I said, sadly. 'For Mum's sake. I did try.'

I'd opened the door to him the day before.

'All right? I'm Ade.'

He was wearing a tight black T-shirt, which was not even slightly appropriate for a man of forty or fifty or whatever he was, and jeans and a huge cracked leather jacket.

'Hello, Ade . . . rian.'

'You Amanda or Katie?'

'Katie.'

'Mind if I come on through, Katie?'

He came on through, his jacket making a creaky noise, and an invisible battle started up between the lunch smell of roast chicken and his very strong aftershave. The chicken was just marching a retreat back to the oven as Amanda emerged from the loo.

'Is that him?'

'Shh,' I said. 'Just watch for a second.'

We stood in the doorway as he went through to the kitchen, kissed Mum, then poured himself a glass of water. He headed straight to the right cupboard and even knew to do the funny twist thing to make the water come out of our dodgy tap.

'What?' hissed Amanda. 'What's the matter?'

'He's been here before.'

'So?'

Was it while I'd been at school? I reran two months' worth of breakfasts, me yabbering away over the Nutella, thinking I had Mum's full attention, while all the time she must have been counting the minutes until she could get rid of me and see Loverboy.

Or had he come round at night? Did Mum wait until

Mands and me were in bed and then sneak out to let him in?

All those times she'd given me McDonald's money to go and meet Lacey in town, had she really been trying to get rid of me?

Judging by the evidence – whose hand was now cupping one of my mother's buttocks – the answer was yes.

Now, there are lots of ways you can spoil a Sunday lunch. You can burn the chicken. You can drop your headphones in the gravy. Or you can sit down across the table from a man with two hairs sprouting out of his nose. By which I mean, the skin on top of his nose. Not his nostrils, which would have been disgusting but at least normal.

'Good chicken, Mum,' I said.

'Yes,' said Amanda.

'It's not too burnt, is it?' said Mum.

'Not at all.'

'It's lovely.'

'Your best ever.'

'It really tastes . . . of . . . chicken.'

There was a pause, which might have lasted a

moment or maybe a hundred years.

'It's delicious,' said Adrian, and then he leaned over and kissed Mum on the mouth. While she was still chewing. With tongues.

After five of the most awkward seconds of my life, he finished eating my mother and went back to his plate. 'So, Amanda, Zoe tells me you play bass?'

'I suppose so,' she said, looking at her lap. 'Sometimes.'

'I used to be in a band once. Back in the day. Split up. Creative differences. You know.'

'Oh, right,' said Amanda.

'Still got a lot of industry connections. You should meet my mate Tony, Tony Topper? The stories he could tell . . .'

'I bet.'

'So, are you any good?'

'I'm . . . OK.'

'Just OK?' Adrian leaned forward and I noticed he had a bit of squashed carrot stuck to his elbow. 'Who are your influences?'

And that was it. For the next ten minutes Amanda was off in Amanda Land, talking about the music she loves and the bands she's going to see and the bands she'd

 19

like to see but can't because they're not touring at the moment or they've split up or they're dead and blah blah infinite blah.

And Adrian was doing it too! For every band she wanted to talk about, he had an actual opinion, which is not what you do when Amanda kicks off on one of her music rants: you keep quiet until it passes. Nose Hairs, on the other hand, was encouraging her. And all the while, Mum was nodding and smiling and stuffing her face with chicken.

'You know,' said Adrian, 'I could do with someone like you in the shop. Vox Vinyl, you know it?'

Amanda nodded like it was Christmas and her birthday and she'd won the lottery. Twice.

'We're a bit short-staffed at the moment, and it's so hard to find someone who knows their stuff. You free to do a few hours next week?'

'I can be,' said Amanda. Honestly, I thought she might faint. I mean, I know she'd always said she fancied working in a record shop, but I hadn't realized it was her Life's Great Ambition. Until now.

'Good stuff,' said Adrian.

'I just have to tell the cafe I'm leaving, but that's

fine – I'm a rubbish waitress anyway.'

'I don't know that we're busy enough to justify you coming over full time . . .'

'That's all right,' said Amanda. 'I'll just . . . I'll be really useful . . . it's fine.'

'Is it?' I said.

At which point, he turned his attention to me. 'I've heard you and your sister like jamming together?' Then he did a little burp. ''Scuse me.'

Mum giggled.

'I've got some instruments kicking around that I've been meaning to sell. Some Gibsons, a couple of Fenders – you'd be welcome to come and mess about with them.'

'That would be amazing!' said Amanda.

I said something that can only be written as 'Mblm'.

'Katie writes songs,' said Amanda. 'About her life and stuff. She's like Lily Allen used to be, sort of. Kooky.'

I'd planned on staying silent but this was too much. 'Don't call me kooky! Kooky is for girls who wear plastic flowers in their hair and have names for their toes.'

'Feisty?'

'No. Feisty says "She's so out there, which is really surprising because she is a girl".'

 21

'Quirky?'

I mimed being sick.

'All right then,' said Amanda. 'How about "different"?'

I thought for a second. 'I will accept different. Thank you.'

There was a very long silence.

'So, Katie, how's school?' said Mum.

'Fine,' I said.

'Tell Adrian what you're studying at the moment.'

'Nothing much.'

'It's OK, Zo. When I was her age, school was the last thing I wanted to think about. Especially on the weekend. Bet you're too busy chasing the boys, yeah, Katie?' Then he winked.

I did my most evil stare. And then I choked on a roast potato.

'It was all pretty grim,' I said to Lacey, as we flumped into our form room. 'So grim that I only managed half my usual portion of trifle. Which is saying something.'

'But you went back for the rest later, right?'

'Of course I did,' I said. 'Things are bad enough; I can't risk malnutrition too.'

 22

'And Amanda's going to be working for him?'

'She's handing in her notice at the cafe today. I tried talking her out of it but all she's interested in is whether he'll give her a staff discount.'

'Mad Jaz alert,' said Lacey, which is our code for when Mad Jaz is in the vicinity. OK, it's not much of a code.

'What's she doing here? I thought Jaz was done with school?'

'Look! Nicole's filming her. This should be good.'

We watched as Jaz opened a can of Fanta and poured it into Ms McAllister's top drawer. Then, like she'd finished her work for the day, she turned around and left.

'She is so mad,' said Lacey. 'And that is such a waste of Fanta.'

'What is?'

'Katie? Earth to Katie?'

'Adrian drinks Fanta,' I said.

'You need to forget about him,' said Lacey. 'Focus on Savannah's party. Or writing a song. Or your new fringe.'

But I couldn't. He was all I could think about. How, when we went for a walk in the park, Mum and Adrian had held hands. And how, when Adrian took Amanda into his shop to show her how to work the till, she was so excited she'd given him a hug.

And, last night, when it got later and later and later, and Adrian didn't leave and didn't leave and didn't leave, and at midnight, when I knew he was next door in Mum's room, in her bed, all I could think about were those two nose hairs lurking, just a metre away, in the dark.

Autocorrect

You ask if I've finished and I say can you wait
But before I can stop you you're clearing my plate
You ask am I happy and I say I'm trying
Your voice says that's great but your eyes know I'm lying

I guess if you want to earn my respect
Can you maybe turn off the autocorrect?

When you talk to your folks I couldn't be better
The undisputed star of your epic Christmas letter
My behaviour's amazing, my grades are great, too
It's kind of a pity that none of it's true

I get that there's stuff that you have to protect
But please can we turn off the autocorrect?

It's late and I'm lonely and though you're next door
There's nothing to link us but walls and a floor
I don't want to lose you but I know I might
No way will we talk when he's here for the night

Mum, if you want me and you to connect
You will have to turn off the autocorrect.

CHAPTER THREE

After that, Adrian was always *there*. Leaving his stupid jacket on top of the washing basket or using the kitchen table as an imaginary drum kit.

'You do like him, don't you?' said Mum, on one of the very few occasions where he wasn't standing next to her.

'Um, yeah,' I said, which was about as positive as I could manage.

'Because –'

'It's just –'

We'd both started at the same time.

'You go,' I said.

'What were you going to say?'

I'd been going to say that I thought it was all going a bit fast, but Mum had a funny look on her face so I decided I'd let her finish.

'It's just, we were thinking, we might move in together. He's here most of the time anyway!'

I did a few fish gulps before I managed, 'But . . . there's

not enough room. Hasn't he got ten million records or something?'

'Ten thousand. But there's plenty of space for them. And us. You girls have a room each. And there's a proper kitchen, and a garden. With a shed. And a pond, sort of. Either a pond or a drainage problem, it depends how you want to look at it.'

'Hang on . . . We're all moving somewhere new? Together? As in, us and him? Sharing a house? And . . . a bathroom?' I don't know why this was the most horrifying thing to me, but it really was.

'Actually,' said Mum, 'our bedroom has its very own bathroom. I don't think even your father's place has that. Not that you're to tell him. Well, maybe you can.'

'I did, last night,' said Amanda.

'Is everyone in on this except me? Because it's starting to feel like some kind of conspiracy.'

'Of course it isn't,' said Mum.

'Then how come Amanda already knows?'

'I suppose I might have mentioned it to her. But look, it's not definite yet . . .'

'Mum showed me pictures,' said Amanda, 'and it's nice. Well, it could be.'

'The lady who had it died, and it's so cheap,' said Mum, digging into her handbag, probably so that she wouldn't have to look at me. 'Adrian reckons—'

I was about to launch into a proper speech about taking things slowly and thinking of others. And was she absolutely sure? And even if she was, maybe she ought to at least check that everyone else in the household was on board. Only, before I could, the man himself came barging in.

'What?' I said. 'What is it that *Adrian reckons*?'

'About what?' he said, looking from me to Mum. She waved a crumpled bit of paper at him, and I spotted an upside-down photo of a house.

He grinned. 'Ah! The place is a bargain, Katie. A real gem. If we move fast we can get it before anyone else even knows about it.'

'Isn't it exciting?' said Mum.

Going to live with Nose Hairs in the house of a dead lady.

'Yaaaay.'

'Bye-bye, geese,' I said.

Turns out that time flies even when you're not having

fun, because before I'd begun to get my head around all this, it was six weeks later, and my last ever walk home from school.

'Bye-bye, footbridge. Bye-bye, old mattress.'

'I can't believe you're going to be getting the bus with the bus lot,' said Lacey. 'They're messed up.'

'Thanks for being so supportive.'

'What can I say?' said Lacey, who clearly knew completely what it was she was going to say, and was about to carry on saying it. 'You've got Finlay, who has the mental age of a six-year-old. Then there's the year sevens, like, about a billion of them. And Nicole from year ten.'

'At least she's interesting,' I said.

'Apparently she got her ear pierced last week, right at the top, with this really tiny stud. Only it swelled up in the night and the stud part disappeared into her ear, like her skin had eaten it. She had to go to A&E and get it taken out. Mad Jaz filmed the whole thing and put it online.'

'That is so disgusting,' I said. 'Have you seen it?'

We slowed down so that Lacey could show me. The camera went right in close and there was even a bit of blood. It finished with Jaz giving the nurse a high five.

 29

'Eighty-seven views,' said Lacey. 'Honestly, who watches this stuff?'

'I know.'

'In fact, I think Jaz gets the bus, too.'

'No she doesn't,' I said, because a dose of Mad Jaz was the last thing I needed. Mad Jaz with her gothy clothes and pale skin, like she's some dead lady from a hundred years ago who crawled out of the grave in order to hang around looking spooky and make snarky comments.

'She does,' said Lacey. 'Poor you.'

Which was much more like it.

'Exactly,' I said. 'It's like, the divorce was the worst thing in the world and we'd just managed to get through that, and then Nose Hairs comes along and now I'm bussing it with Jaz. Poor, poor me.'

'Poor you,' said Lacey. 'Hey, so Paige and Sofie had a row over who got to buy these navy slingbacks in Topshop and they're not speaking. So Savannah's uninvited them both to her party until they sort it out.'

Sometimes I think that Lacey isn't quite as fascinated by my problems as she should be.

'Honestly. Who even cares about shoes?'

'Not you, apparently,' said Lacey, staring at

my scuffed Doc Martens.

'Lace, can't you just be nice for five more minutes? We are never going to do this walk again, and I don't want my last memory of our time together to be of you trolling my footwear.'

She blew her fringe out of her eyes. 'I'm just grumpy because I'm going to miss you. OK?'

Oh.

'Don't say that! We'll still see each other all day. And we can talk to each other on the phone the entire way in, so it'll basically be like we're walking together.'

'I suppose.'

She stopped under the tree with the picnic bench where we'd sometimes share a Magnum.

'What?' I said.

'Nothing,' said Lacey. 'Just . . .'

She looked kind of worried, standing there, her white blonde hair blowing in the cold breeze that always comes off the water, and I wondered whether she'd planned for something unfortunate to happen as a leaving present.

That's the problem with Lacey: she's not the best judge of this kind of thing. She could just as easily have got me a special Magnum as she could have arranged for the boys to chuck me into the canal.

I readied myself, and then . . .

'Surprise,' she said, awkwardly, and pulled a little box out of her bag.

'What?' I said.

'Open it.'

So I did, carefully, and . . .

'Lace!'

My best friend had lined the box in violet tissue paper, my favourite colour, and filled it with . . .

'It's mementos of our best walks. There's the party popper, from your birthday – I saved it. And the song we made up about the geese babies. I know you've forgotten it so I wrote it down . . .'

'And a pair of Magnum sticks!'

My insides went as warm and gooey as a chocolate pudding. In fact, I was starting to think of a new song, maybe called something like 'Walking With You', about friendship, and memories, and how beautiful it all was, when Lacey said:

'Other surprise!'

At which point the whole rest of the canal crowd jumped out from behind the tree and dumped me in the water.

 32

▶

I got myself home and dried off and sat down on my bed, surrounded by boxes, some of which I hadn't even unpacked from the last move, and thank goodness I had my stereo because otherwise I think I might have exploded or crumbled or something.

That's what I love about music. There's always a song that knows how you're feeling.

I played 'Back to Black', over and over, Tom Waits, some Leonard Cohen, lots of Patty Griffin and Joni Mitchell. It was as I was listening to 'Blue' for the third time that there was a gentle knock on my door.

'What?'

'I bring word from the rest of us,' said Amanda.

'Which is?'

'MESSAGE RECEIVED, OK? We know you don't want to move, but can this soundtrack of extreme misery please stop?'

She was kind of smiling as she said it, and even though I really did not want to, I found myself smiling too. 'All right. But only as a favour to you.'

'Play me that tune again,' said Amanda. 'The happy one you were doing a few weeks ago. Dah–dah–dah–daaaaah?'

I played it, and it sounded . . . hopeful. So I played it again.

'Does it have words?' said Amanda.

It hadn't. Now, though, with Mands next to me, I tried:

> I've got mad skin
> I've got mad hair
> I borrowed your stuff and I don't even care

'What did you borrow?' said Amanda.

'Your yellow jumper. Deal with it, sister,' I said, leaning over to scribble in my lyric book. 'Go grab your guitar? I want to hear it with a bassline.'

Amanda got her guitar and sat down to pick it out, carefully, precisely, Amandaishly.

'Like that but faster,' I said. 'Speed it up a bit.'

Which she did, and I sang:

> I've got mad skin
> I've got mad hair
> I borrowed your stuff and I don't even care
> I'm the big bad apple on the family tree
> Deal with it, sister, that's just me

'I like that,' said Amanda. 'And I would also like my jumper back.'

We played it a few more times.

'Is there any more?' said Amanda.

'It's a work in progress,' I said. 'I've just been finding it . . . hard.'

'I do get it, you know,' said Amanda.

'You nearly do,' I said. 'There's just that funny bit towards the end, it needs a pause after "*Deal with it, sister*". You're rushing.'

'I meant about the move. I'm nervous as well. And so's Mum. It's *not* just you, Katie. It isn't easy for any of us.'

I leaned over to get another line into my book before it evaporated.

'We're all finding it hard.'

'Then why are we doing it?' I asked. 'Can't we just wait a few months?'

Mands thrummed a bit on her guitar. 'Maybe Mum wants to get going with the rest of her life. The divorce went on long enough.'

'Yeah,' I said, because it had.

'We'll move,' said Amanda, 'and we'll unpack, and then everything will get back to normal.'

 35

'I suppose,' I said. Then, 'Want to see something funny?' And I showed her the video of Nicole's ear.

'Eeeurgh! How have eight and a half thousand people watched that?'

'Have they?' I looked at the view-counter, and they had. 'Wow. It's gone totally viral.'

We were silent for a second, thinking of all the people out there watching a close-up of Nicole's ear, then sending it to their friends. Or maybe their enemies, because it really was disgusting. If one person sent it to two people, then they each sent it to two people, then each of *them* sent it to two people . . .

'But why?' said Amanda. Then, 'Will you forward me the link? Adrian will love it.'

CHAPTER FOUR

'So what's it like?' said Lacey, the day we moved into the new house.

I was about to tell her that the mobile reception was rubbish, but then my phone went and hung up on her, so I suppose that said it for me.

Our new house was great. In a sort of really dark, horrible kind of a way, where the floors creaked and everything smelt a bit mouldy and the windows didn't open properly and when you did get them unstuck you couldn't shut them again.

And when I went out to explore, all the neighbours were about eighty and said things like 'Good morning' and 'Nice day to wash the car' and 'Watch where you're going, young lady', just because I happened to be walking and texting at the same time, which is completely normal everywhere else and it's hardly my fault that mobility scooters can't get out of the way.

Adrian had stuck his drum kit right under my bedroom window, so even after I'd unpacked my boxes and put all my things out, the room still didn't feel like mine. All I could see were heaps of flattened cardboard and cymbals and walls the colour of wee.

I thought I'd write a song about it, but the wee thing made it sound like the whole situation was funny and it wasn't. At all.

Then I tried finishing 'Just Me'. I had two verses, but no ending. And after half an hour I still had no ending, just a whole heap of things that didn't rhyme with other things and a sore brain.

So instead, I tried moving the wardrobe over a bit, in case that helped things.

At which point the wardrobe door fell off on to my actual face.

'Mum? Muuum!'

It wasn't Mum who appeared outside my bedroom door but Adrian.

'Your mother can't come upstairs right now. She's having a sit-down.'

'Why?'

'She's had a small electric shock.'

'From what?'

'The oven.'

'Do ovens usually give people electric shocks?'

Adrian looked a bit uncomfortable. 'Not usually, no.'

Our thoughtful moment was interrupted by Amanda, who was looking flushed and upset and distinctly non-Amandaish.

'It's fine, but I was looking under my bed for my hairbrush, I can't find it anywhere, and I saw a mouse. Well, mice, I suppose – three mice. At least three mice.'

'What do you mean, "at least"?'

'They go quite fast,' said Amanda. 'And I didn't want to look at them properly, because they were mice.'

'Probably pets left behind by the last lot who were here.'

'The dead lady?' I said. 'Maybe they came out of her CORPSE.'

'Katie!'

So we sat down and had our first ever family gathering, to list all the things that were wrong with the house. It went like this:

- strange smell (even after opening the windows)
- windows that open but don't close again
- a quite big hole in the floor of the airing cupboard

- oven is electrified
- mice
- the loo flushes with hot water (two words: poo soup).

'It's not so bad,' said Amanda, in a way that made it clear that even Miss Optimism thought it was bad.

'I'll talk to the estate agent,' said Adrian, tapping out the world's slowest text message with one of his massive thumbs. He stared at his phone. 'It's not sending. Why won't it send?'

'There's reception if you lean right the way out of the window so it feels like you might be about to fall out,' I said helpfully. 'Or, at the end of the drive.' And off he went.

The rest of us stared at each other.

'Did you not notice any of this when you came to look around?' I asked Mum, trying to make it come out light and non-accusing.

'We only went round quickly,' she said. 'It was such a bargain . . .'

She looked all small and hopeless and I wanted to roar at the universe for being so mean.

'We'll sort it out,' said Amanda cheerfully. 'Really, it'll

be fine. Better than fine. We're all in this together.'

'I'm going for a walk,' I said.

'Now?'

'To see the bus stop. Since I'm going to have to be there tomorrow morning anyway.'

I left them to it and went off down the driveway, past Adrian on his phone, past Manda's hairbrush, which I went back and retrieved from the recycling heap, and off into the sunshine.

Now, I want to be clear that what I am about to say does not in any way mean that I was happy or that I liked the new place or that I wanted to be there.

It was just . . . there was something quite nice about walking down the driveway and along the pavement with the grass smelling green and fresh, all beaded with drops of rain and glimmering in the light. Hardly any cars came past, and the sky felt high and open, empty and waiting to be filled.

I let loose a few bars of 'Just Me', and it sounded even better outside. Especially after I adjusted the melody very, very slightly and sent the last verse spiralling up towards the watery sun.

I've got mad love
I've got mad hate
I've got my whole life to come and I just
   can't wait
And here's the thing, I think you'll agree
We're all in this together. It's not just me.

The words fell into place like they'd been there all along.

I did a twirl and then another. There's nothing quite like using a hairbrush as a microphone, is there? And then . . .

'Are you all right, dear?'

There was the bus stop. Complete with two old ladies.

My face was hotter than the sun. Hotter than the sun on fire. Which I think it is anyway, but still.

'You have a lovely voice,' said the nearest one. Then, to her friend: 'Doesn't she have a lovely voice?'

'She's the one who barged into my scooter,' said the other lady.

'Oh *is* she?' said old lady number one, at which point I decided to turn around and go home.

Down the end of the drive my phone started going in my pocket. When I saw who it was, my heartbeat went syncopated, which is fun when it's music but biologically speaking, probably not the best.

'Dad!'

'We're just taking five, so I thought I'd check in on my special girl.'

It's the miracle of phones that even though he was stateside, his voice sounded so clear that if I shut my eyes I could pretend he was standing just behind me, his hands on my shoulders, holding me close.

'I'm all right,' I said. 'We've just moved into the new house.'

'And . . . ?'

'It's fine,' I said, because, on reflection, I didn't want to spend my precious Dad minutes on anything even slightly Adrian. 'How's California?'

'All good.'

'Hot?'

'Oh yes. You really must visit.'

'You know Mum won't let me come in term-time.'

'Honestly, your mother! You can't be doing anything important.'

'Only homework.'

'Exactly,' he said.

'Or,' I said, trying to keep the hope out of my voice, and failing, 'you could always come here? We have loads of space now.'

'Soon,' he said. 'Work's pretty busy at the moment, but soon.'

Dad's a session musician, which is the coolest of the cool. He's an amazing guitarist, plus he also plays bass and the keyboard and the clarinet, although I have no evidence for the last one and he does have a tendency to exaggerate.

Even so, he's basically the best musician in the world and I'm not just saying that because we share chromosomes. You can hear him on zillions of tracks, from cereal adverts to stuff by very major rock stars who I'm not allowed to name because it's supposed to be them playing, not him.

The only difficult thing about Dad being so awesome is that his work is not very regular, so when he does get offered a job, he kind of needs to take it.

'I'm still planning on coming over just before Christmas,' he said.

'Of course. And Christmas isn't that far away.'

'Only a few months.'

And for all the magic of mobiles, I could feel the whole distance between us. Every last millimetre.

'Written anything good lately?'

'I'm working on a couple of things,' I told him. 'Hey, what did you think of the last batch?'

'Oh, fantastic. All of it.'

'Really?' My heart did another flip. 'I wasn't sure about "Wet Weather". But if you like it . . .'

'I love it,' said Dad. 'The lyrics are phenomenal. Your best yet.'

'"Wet Weather" was the instrumental number. The one with a ripply bit at the beginning that was supposed to sound like rain . . . ?'

'Of course it was. And I thought it was amazing.'

Now it was a good thing we were on the phone, or he'd have seen me cry. 'Thank you, Dad.'

'I've got to go back into the studio now, sweetheart. Sorry this is such a quick one. You take care, won't you?'

'I will. And Dad—'

At which point the stupid, stupid, stupid reception cut out, and he'd gone.

So I stomped back up the driveway, and then I trod on a

snail and felt bad and tried to walk a bit more delicately and then trod on another snail anyway which just goes to show that sometimes there really is no point to anything.

And then I thought about getting the bus with Finlay, and Nicole and Mad Jaz, and my mood got even worse, if that's possible, which it was.

We'd started calling her Mad Jaz as a sort of joke, although it isn't that much of a joke because Jaz has a tendency to go crazy.

Like, once there was this spate of muggings on the high street and we had a policeman come in to show us self-defence. He needed a volunteer to demonstrate his techniques and picked Jaz and, to cut a long (and violent) story short, Jaz ended up being arrested.

I'd been staying well away from our resident psycho-goth, which luckily had been quite easy to do, because Jaz seemed to have taken the decision to stop coming to lessons. Which, now I thought about it, meant that she almost certainly wouldn't be getting the bus any more. After all, why would you bother going to school if you weren't planning to be in any classes?

I came through the front door to find that everyone had mysteriously vanished.

'Hello? Hello?'

Nothing. Just some distant guitar noise.

'Manda?'

I went upstairs and across the landing.

The door to Mum's bedroom – no, not Mum's bedroom, Mum *and Adrian's* bedroom – was open, but there wasn't anyone in there. Just the faint scent of Mum's eau de toilette and the not-so-faint stench of Adrian's deodorant.

So I knocked on Amanda's door. 'Manda?'

He was there. Sitting on a chair by her bed, guitar under one arm. 'Hey, Katie.'

'Oh. Hello.'

Amanda was propped against her desk, head bent over the frets. She didn't meet my eye. 'Katie.'

'What are you two doing?' It came out more confrontational than I'd meant. But surely Amanda couldn't have been playing with . . . him . . .

I mean, there was making the guy feel at home and then there was out-and-out sisterly betrayal.

Playing together was *ours*. We'd done it with Dad since we were tiny – Mands banging a drum while I sat on his knee and he held my fingers in place on the strings. We got older and better, and there were nights, after a

 47

really big row, when music was just about the only thing keeping us together.

And now here she was, strumming away as if it was just normal.

'We're not doing anything,' said Amanda, as Adrian said:

'You'll like this . . .'

'She won't,' said Amanda, actually putting her fingers across his strings to stop him from playing. Quite right, too.

While Amanda had at least noticed that she was in trouble, Adrian was still grinning. 'Go on, Katie, grab your guitar; we could do with your expertise here.'

'My fingers are tired,' I said, which made no sense whatsoever, but there you go.

'So are mine,' said Amanda quickly. 'Shall we call it a night?'

Adrian's head swivelled between us, then he picked up his guitar and left, pausing to call, 'I'll put on a pepperoni pizza, shall I?'

'Katie . . .' Amanda began.

'No, it's fine,' I said, heading for the door. 'You play with him, if it makes you happy.'

'Really?' said Amanda.

'NO.'

Mobility Scooting on the Pavement

Got a head full of blame
And a knee full of hurt
Got a heart full of shame
And a face full of dirt

Lady,
You'd think you'd have a bell
Or perhaps a kinda hooter
Somewhere on your mobility scooter

You're a Blue Badge holder
And I was in your way
One day I'll get older
But first I need to say

Lady,
Get yourself a bell
And a really massive hooter
And fit them on to your mobility scooter

And if you won't do that
Then lighten my load
And ride the stupid thing
Along the stupid road.

CHAPTER FIVE

Turning up at a bus stop on a school morning is a bit like jumping into a den of tigers. Or something just as deadly, but not so endangered. Like jumping into a bowl of cashews, if you've got a nut allergy.

To avoid making it totally obvious to the bus crowd that I was Katie-no-mates, I made sure I got there nice and early. Which didn't work at all, as, in fact, I was the first one to arrive. I ended up standing around completely on my own, fiddling with my phone.

OK, not fiddling. Trying to call Lacey so we'd at least be able to talk to each other on our way in, like we'd planned. But her phone just rang and rang and rang.

She probably had it on silent, or something.

Which left me with a dilemma – how many times should you try calling a person before you start to seem a bit crazy? I stopped after fifteen attempts, and went back to staring out at the road. I couldn't even try to look cool, as it was guitar lesson day. I had to stand there with this

 50

huge thing strapped to my back, like a kind of deformed tortoise.

Then, suddenly, just a few minutes before the bus was supposed to turn up, it was the Harltree version of Piccadilly Circus.

A bunch of year sevens were messing about with a pack of cards. Nicole was fiddling with a lighter while Finlay did something grim to an egg sandwich.

And I thought of Lacey, and was about to try calling her again, when . . .

'All right, Katie?'

Oh no.

'Jaz!'

'What are you doing here?'

Out on the street she looked scarier than ever, the spots on her chin oozing yellow stuff, and double piercings in both ears.

'I'm getting the bus now,' I said.

'Why?' Jaz was wearing a school skirt, but instead of the regulation navy blue sweatshirt, she had a black bodice type thing with sleeves that billowed out at the top, then narrowed from her elbows to her wrists and did up with rows of tiny buttons. This, combined with a fairly extreme level of make-up, made her look like a twisted Victorian doll.

'Because Mum has just bought the world's worst house with the world's worst man and . . .'

I tailed off because it was possible that Jaz wasn't quite listening. I could tell because she had turned her back on me and because she had started talking to Nicole. Which was all fine by me.

My plan had been to stay safely downstairs, near the driver, but just as we were getting on, Jaz put her face right in mine and said, 'You can sit with us.'

And suddenly I was pining for the good old days when it had just been me, the bus stop and my guitar.

Two minutes later, and we were at the back of the top deck: Finlay and the year sevens shoving themselves between the seats, Nicole in the middle, plucking her eyebrows with what looked like a pair of pliers, and Jaz in the back corner, like some kind of public-transport-based royalty.

'Katie?'

'Um, yes?'

'Finlay is trying to open your guitar case.'

 52

I turned around, and he was.

'Oh. Thanks, Jaz.'

Mad Jaz was being nice. Weirdy weird.

'I don't think I've ever seen you without Lacey. It's like you're joined at the hip or something.'

'Nah,' I said, thinking of the zillion missed calls Lace would be finding the very second she looked at her phone. 'We're not actually even that friendly any more. You know. People move on. Apparently.'

'Do you want me to get Finlay to egg her?' said Jaz.

And in fact, I was so upset at Lacey not phoning me back that I almost thought about saying yes, only at that exact second my phone rang and it was her.

'Lace! Where've you been all my life?'

'Oh, you know.' She sounded distant. In all the ways you can be distant. 'We were walking along.'

'You and who?'

'Just . . . people.'

I considered bringing up our pact to talk to each other on the phone, and then decided it would sound needy and that I wouldn't say anything about it.

'It's just . . . I thought we were going to talk, on the way in. Like we'd said.'

'Sorry. Something came up.'

'Well . . .' *Just leave it, Katie. She clearly isn't interested. Let her go.* 'Want to come over tonight and see the House of Horrors? We've got mice and everything.'

'Maybe.'

'Oh go on. I'll make Mum give us money for Chinese takeaway. The chow mein's on me, girlfriend.'

'Chow mein?' The reply was immediate, and very enthusiastic. Unfortunately, it hadn't come from Lacey. It had come from Mad Jaz. 'I like chow mein. And Nicole likes it too.'

And suddenly I was down to host the world's scariest sleepover.

'Um, Lace, ring me back in a sec, OK?'

I put the phone straight down and was about to explain that it hadn't been a general invitation, only I found that Jaz was going through the contents of my bag like that was a completely normal thing to do.

'Ha ha, look – it's Katie's secret diary.'

Of course, she'd found my lyric book. People like Jaz can smell that kind of thing a mile off.

'No, it's not.'

She flicked it open. '"Just Me". What is this, please?'

Only Jaz could make the word 'please' sound like a threat.

'I write songs.'

'Seriously?'

'Yes.'

'Since when?'

I thought back, and realized, which was quite interesting, that I couldn't ever remember *not* having written them. The song for Manda's fifteenth birthday, which had made her cry, even though she pretended it was an allergic reaction to her new mascara. The divorce songs, which made *me* cry. And the ones about silly stuff, like types of breakfast cereal and the weather and never being able to find shoes that look nice and that I can also walk in. Actually, that last one isn't silly at all; it's very important.

'Since forever.'

I genuinely couldn't tell whether Jaz thought this was good or bad. Her face was pretty hard to read, what with it being covered in eyeliner and cakey foundation, which was supposed to hide her acne but in fact just made it look like acne under a layer of foundation.

'Sing one, then.'

She said it in this laid-back, not-bothered kind of a way, so quietly that I'd almost have ignored it, only when I looked up her eyes were staring right into mine. Like it was a test.

'Really? It's not like they're any good, Jaz. You won't be that interested, they're just stuff I do when I'm—'

'*Sing one.*'

So there I was, new on the bus, surrounded by year sevens, Finlay, and Nicole. And a load of people who were going into work or wherever it is that adults go on a bus at eight in the morning, which I suppose must be work because otherwise you'd stay in bed. There were drips running down the insides of the windows, and the air smelt like diesel and morning breath.

Not exactly an ideal environment for my very first public performance.

Which I was about to point out, only then I realized I was actually more scared of what Jaz would say if I *didn't* sing than if I did.

So I took a deep breath, and then another one, as though I was standing at the top of the high-diving board at the leisure centre. Except that's a poor example, because I've never managed to jump.

But I did sing.

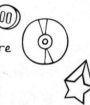

I've got mad skin
I've got mad hair
I borrowed your stuff and I don't even care
I'm the big bad apple on the family tree
Deal with it, sister, that's just me

And . . . it was OK. Better than OK.

I've got mad beats
I've got mad moves
I know your mum really disapproves
If you're up for a laugh then you're my cup of tea
Friends forever, that's just me

I could feel, without even having to look, that everyone was listening, leaning in, as if my words were a sort of a net, drawing them all together, and, for maybe a minute or two, the whole bus faded away.

I've got mad love
I've got mad hate
I've got my whole life to come and I
  just can't wait
And here's the thing, I think you'll agree
We're all in this together. It's not just me.

I finished, and in the pause just after, I saw a new light in Jaz's eyes. Because I'd done it. I'd opened myself up, taken a risk – and earned her respect.

She opened her mouth slowly, her surprisingly pink tongue running across her bottom lip.

'Katie?'

'Yes?'

'Finlay just dropped your phone out the window.'

CHAPTER SIX

I'm going to try to be very calm about this and not go over the top or anything, so all I will say is that it was like the world had ended, and leave it at that.

Just getting my phone back into my hand was hard enough, on an alien bus in the middle of who-knows-where. And when I did, the screen was cracked and the back was mashed and it wouldn't turn on.

I cradled it in my arms, hoping it knew how much I'd loved it.

'Finlay, you are annoying,' said Jaz.

So it wasn't shaping up to be the best of days.

There was a bit of a moment when I came into the form room with the bus lot, and Lacey was there with the canal crowd. I was going to talk to her, but somehow a load of boys got in between us and by the time I'd squished past we were all on our way into assembly.

Then we were in the hall but not next to each other, which had never happened in the whole history of Katie and Lacey. Not that I minded or anything. I mean, I knew we'd have to sit apart eventually. I suppose. I just hadn't thought it would happen quite so soon.

'So, for my birthday,' Savannah was saying, as we shuffled back out after twenty minutes of some woman talking about protecting bats, 'I'm thinking I'd like a MacBook, a pair of diamond studs and as much Clarins stuff as they'll give me. Plus Glastonbury tickets. Because of my creative spirit. Dad will take me.'

Well, where to start? The idea of Savannah at Glastonbury was so spectacularly hilarious that I almost didn't say anything, just so that she'd go and I could hear about it afterwards. But that would have meant denying someone else the chance to go. Someone like Manda. Or me.

'Savannah, do you know what Glastonbury *is*?'

She ran her fingers through her advert-blonde hair. 'Katie, how can you not know? It's this amazing party where Cara Delevingne and Alexa Chung go to drink champagne and wear Hunter wellies.' Her head flicked round to Paige. 'I should ask for Hunter wellies, too.'

'So you're OK with sleeping in a tent,' I said.

'I'd stay in a hotel, babes.'

'I don't think there is one. I think you have to sleep

 60

in a tent and use a chemical toilet. And, honestly, it's mainly about listening to music. You know, bands. While standing outside. Even when it's raining. And it usually does.'

'Eew. How do Cara's brows cope? OK, not Glastonbury. Maybe I'll get a Miss Sixty bag instead. Would that honour my creative spirit, do we think? The new season is pretty out there . . .'

All the way through this I'd been trying to catch Lacey's eye, but she was deep in conversation with Sofie and then it was time for my guitar lesson.

The story goes that when I was four I found Dad's guitar and started playing on it. Mum discovered me plucking out a reasonably decent version of the *Coronation Street* theme tune, and together they decided that I was some kind of prodigy and that I ought to have lessons.

The funny (not in a ha ha way) thing about this is that I'm not a prodigy, or anything like one. I'm pretty rubbish. In my head, there's Jimmy Page making it sound like his fingers are taking an actual stairway to heaven, and then there's the reality, which is Katie Cox mashing up chords in a Portakabin.

'I've got something I'd like to finish off this week,' I said to Jill, my guitar teacher, as I unzipped my case, half expecting to find an egg sandwich nestling into the strings.

She was fine with that, so I sat down and played 'Just Me', stopping every time it sounded less than perfect, which was mostly.

If you're up for a laugh then you're my cup of tea
Friends forever, that's just me

'No. That's not right. It needs something else.'

'Maybe just hold the E for a moment longer?' said Jill.

I tried it, and it was better.

I've got mad beats
I've got mad moves
I know that your mum really disapproves
If you're up for a laugh then you're my cup of tea
Friends forever, that's just me

I faltered, and, as usual, my hands wouldn't do quite what I needed them to . . . *'That's just me. J-just me. Just me.'* The notes fell away from my fingers. 'Sorry.'

'Katie, it's really good.'

'Well –' I was so embarrassed that I thought my cheeks were going to melt and start dripping on to the carpet – 'thank you. Can I have one more go?'

'Um,' said Jill, 'you've been here nearly an hour, and in theory it's only a twenty-minute lesson, so . . .'

'What?! Why didn't you say anything?'

Jill mumbled some stuff about talent that was just her covering up the fact that she was too sweet to chuck me out.

So I cut her off and raced to the canteen, where, thank goodness, Lacey was waiting for me.

'Good lesson?'

'It was fine.' I didn't really want to get into my extended one-woman show. 'Anyway,' I said, ultra-casually. 'What did I miss this morning? I bet loads of stuff happened.'

'When?'

'When you were walking along the canal. While I was getting the bus from our new house for the first time ever. A bus I was on with Mad Jaz . . . I'm sure there's loads of things you need to be telling me so I'll shut up about everything going on in my life and let you talk.'

 63

'Devi Lester has these new trainers. He kept going on and on about how expensive they were so Kai pulled one off and kicked it on to a barge.'

'Wow. That sounds a bit like something that happened to me on the bus this morning –'

'And when Devi went to get it back this woman came out and screamed at him . . .'

'Because Jaz started going through my bag –'

'And so he waited until she'd gone inside and tried to hook it out with a branch but he couldn't reach. So he's going back later with a hockey stick.'

'It was really intimidating. I just didn't know how to stop her.'

Lacey looked up from dissecting her sandwich. 'Jaz was upsetting you?'

'Yeah.'

'Then how come you came in together? Why stay with her, if she's so intimidating?'

'I wasn't "with her",' I said. 'We just happened to be standing next to each other.'

She shrugged. 'So am I coming back to yours later, then?'

'If you like,' I said.

'Do you want me to?'

'Yeah, but no pressure.'

'Cos I don't have to come.'

'LACEY,' I said, possibly a little bit more loudly than was strictly necessary because a load of other people turned around and stared at us. 'Please will you come to my house tonight and watch *Mean Girls*?'

'All right,' said Lacey. 'No need to be weird about it.'

At which point everything got better again.

School ended and Lacey and I walked to the bus stop, where Finlay didn't seem to notice us at all, and when the bus came we sat downstairs, at the back, which was possibly the worst seat, what with all the darkness and diesel fumes and being jolted every time we went over a bump. Only, with Lace next to me, sharing a Curly Wurly, it was like we were in our own little nest. No one knew we were there.

'So you didn't answer my calls because you were afraid they'd throw your phone in the water,' I said. All things considered it did sound reasonable.

'And you didn't answer when I rang you back because your phone got broken.'

I lifted its poor sad body out of my bag and on to my lap.

'It's no good, I can't look.'

'Maybe we should bury it in your garden.'

'Not the best final resting place,' I said, thinking of the nettles and the pool of grey sludge. 'It was a good phone; it deserves more.'

Out of the window I saw that we'd pulled away from all the nice roads full of houses and shops and postboxes and other useful things and were heading out towards the fields.

'Hey, this is our stop.'

And so we came tumbling off the bus, me and Lacey and a broken phone and a guitar, ready for a bit of full-on friendship.

To find Nicole and Jaz waiting for us.

CHAPTER SEVEN

Don't panic, I told myself.

'We've got big plans for tonight,' said Jaz. 'Nicole wants to pierce her thumbnail. So we borrowed a staple gun from the art room. Well, not borrowed, exactly . . .'

'I didn't know you were invited,' said Lacey, and she didn't seem too pleased.

At which point I was desperate to tell her that, in fact, the person who'd invited Jaz was Jaz.

Only I couldn't because the person standing next to me was Jaz.

'So, where's your new place then?' Jaz said, and all I could do was start walking there, and hope that she and Nicole would get a better offer somewhere along the way. Which meant within the next four minutes.

Lacey wasn't saying anything at all. And Jaz had her headphones on, nodding away to music so loud that it was managing to drown out the traffic. Part of me wanted her to switch it off so I could make another excuse and get her to go away, but most of me wanted her to keep listening because then I wouldn't have to speak to her.

We got to my front door.

'Are you sure you want to come in?' I said. 'It's going to be pretty rubbish, if I'm being honest.'

'I might just head home,' said Lacey.

'Not you, I meant . . .' Only I didn't get to finish the sentence because at that point the front door opened.

'Ladies!'

Apparently, in the moment before you die your whole life flashes before your eyes. Thinking about it, I suppose it can't be your *whole* life. Partly because it would have to go so fast that you wouldn't be able to notice any of it, and also because a lot of the flash would be taken up with things like being asleep and looking very closely at the skin on the back of your hand and leaving voicemail.

'Adrian,' I whispered. 'What are you doing here? You're not due back for another two hours. Minimum.'

'Business was a bit slow, so I thought we'd pack it in for the day.' Adrian grinned. 'Having a party, are you?'

'No!'

'Shame. I was just going to get fish and chips.'

'Yes please,' said Jaz.

Stay calm stay calm stay calm.

 68

'Well?' Amanda was hovering in the hall. 'Are you coming in or what?'

Let's just recap.

- Mad Jaz
- Nicole from year ten
- Adrian
- Amanda
- Lacey
- Me

So we were all sitting down eating fish and chips LIKE EVERYTHING WAS NORMAL AND FINE. Amanda was giving us the fascinating story of how many sales they'd made that day (it was three), and Adrian was telling Mad Jaz all about his days in a band.

'Me and Tony, we were signed and everything. Tony Topper, you know him?'

'Of course she doesn't,' I said.

'Still got my kit. Couldn't bring myself to part with it.'

'Then why is it in *my* bedroom?' I asked.

Adrian launched into a whole thing about how the

leak in his and Mum's room wasn't good for musical instruments, but before he could finish, Jaz's eyes went all glinty and mad.

'Can I have a go, then?'

There was a minuscule pause as Adrian clearly thought about how much he didn't want anyone messing around with his precious drums but also how much he was enjoying having an audience.

'You know what? Katie's been using them as clothes hangers for long enough. We'll set them up, have a jamming session!'

'In my bedroom?' I squeaked. 'There's really no need to go up there, it's incredibly messy, disgusting actually. Why don't we bring the drums downstairs, or we could just leave it . . .'

'Maybe you should have thought about cleaning up a bit before you invited so many people over,' said Amanda, and right then and there I decided that her yellow jumper wouldn't be making its way back into her wardrobe, however much she asked for it.

Despite my many, many objections, we all ended up cramming into my room. Mands started picking out odd notes on her bass in the way she does, while Jaz sat down on the edge of my bed and didn't play the drums so much as physically attack them. Seriously, if I'd been on the receiving end of what she was giving out, I'd have dialled 999.

'Reminds me of the glory days,' said Adrian, who was sitting cross-legged on the floor next to my dirty jeans pile, balancing a keyboard across his crotch. 'Great technique you've got there, Amanda. And Jaz, that's some real . . . energy.'

This pleased Jaz so much that she whacked the biggest drum hard enough to knock it on to the floor.

'You two going to join in?' said Adrian, looking at me and Lacey.

'I can only play the recorder,' said Lacey, in a way that made it clear she didn't even want to do that. Nose Hairs didn't seem to notice her moodiness, though, and offered her a tambourine.

'But I don't . . .' Lacey began. 'I thought we were going to watch *Mean Girls*, Katie. I'm going home.'

This could not be allowed to happen.

'Lacey, please. Let's just get this done, then we'll absolutely watch *Mean Girls*. Promise.'

Very slowly, and in a way that made it clear she found the whole thing properly stupid, Lacey took the tambourine from Adrian, who gave it a little shake as he handed it over. 'Wicked. Nicole?'

In answer, Nicole held up Jaz's phone.

'She's videoing it,' said Jaz. 'For posterity.'

'Yup, yup,' said Adrian. 'Katie?'

This was awful. But on the plus side, if we were playing, then Lacey couldn't fight with me, and Adrian couldn't be too embarrassing. And Jaz couldn't . . . do whatever terrible thing it was that Jaz was surely about to do.

I unzipped my guitar from its case and tuned up.

'Let's go,' said Adrian. 'One, two, three, four –'

There was a minute, maybe two, where the air in my bedroom turned into this music casserole, guitar twangs, drum beats and the tinny notes from the keyboard all floating about together and taking it in turns to come to the surface. It was a complete mess.

Then, Adrian began playing . . .

'That's your song,' said Jaz. 'The one you sang on the bus this morning.'

Exactly how did Adrian know the tune to 'Just Me'?

Then I saw Amanda's guilty face, and I knew.

And she knew that I knew.

'I just went through it with him a couple of times the other night, that's all. It sounded nice with two guitars, and I thought—'

'You played *my* song?' I said. 'You sat down with him and you played something that is mine? With him?'

'Yeah! And we got it pretty good,' said Adrian, who clearly hadn't quite grasped the epic treachery going on right beneath his hairy nose. 'I've worked out a keyboard backing, you do the guitar and vocals, yeah?'

No.

NO.

There was no way I was singing *my* song with the Cox Family Destruction Collective, featuring drums from Mad Jaz. No way.

They were all looking at me.

'I really don't want to,' I said.

They kept looking.

'Seriously.'

More stares.

'I suppose . . .' I said, hopelessly. 'But does it have to be "Just Me"? We could do "Bohemian Rhapsody", or "Yellow Submarine". Or "The Wheels on the Bus" . . .'

'I like *your* song,' said Jaz, and I honestly couldn't tell whether she genuinely did like it or just wanted to see me squirm.

'It's just . . . quite . . . personal,' I said, and Lacey said:

'Not that personal, is it? If you sang it to everyone on the bus.'

There was nothing – and I really mean nothing – I could do. Except maybe get up and walk out, but I didn't think of that until afterwards.

So I hummed the tune, just a bit, and then, in that way that sometimes happens, the music sort of took over and I hummed it louder.

'Cool, cool,' said Adrian, nodding his head to the beat.

Then Jaz started playing at the exact speed of the song, *boom tish, boom boom tish*, like she'd been a drummer all her life. Which, come to think of it, was perfectly possible.

'Nice,' said Adrian, and together we sort of mashed through the song, stopping every now and then for Amanda to twiddle, or for Jaz to get a bit overenthusiastic, which was often.

'Again?' said Adrian, and we did it again, and this time it almost sounded quite good.

'Well, this has been fun,' I said. 'Shall we call it a night?'

'Once more,' said Adrian. 'And this time, you should sing.'

'Nah.'

'If you don't,' said Adrian, 'then I will. *I'm the something apple in the fa-mi-ly . . .*'

Hearing him singing my words, or at least a version of them, was deeply cringe-inducing. As if I'd come home to find him trying on my clothes.

'It's *I'm the big bad apple on the family tree*,' I said.

'Sing it,' said Adrian, and Amanda said:

'Oh, go on, Katie.'

Ages and ages ago I remember we did this poem in English, something about choosing between two paths. And how once you go down one path your life changes forever and you can never go back and see what was down the other path. I think there was a difficult bit about leaves and undergrowth in there too, which I never quite understood.

Anyway, the point being that sometimes you have these major moments that decide loads of stuff, not just for a bit, but forever.

Now, given how things turned out, I'd like to say that I knew I was having one of those moments as Lacey,

Amanda, Mad Jaz, Nicole and Adrian all paused, and looked at me.

Honestly, though, it wasn't like that at all. Jaz and Adrian came in on the intro, Mands picked up the bassline, Nicole held out the phone, and I just opened my mouth and sang.

Because singing is what I do.

> I've got mad skin
> I've got mad hair
> I borrowed your stuff and I don't even care

It started out fairly quiet and I could feel everyone settling into their instruments while my voice kind of floated around somewhere up above. Like a feather or a kite, or the time Paige made Lacey's maths homework into a paper aeroplane and sailed it off the top of the science lab.

> I'm the big bad apple on the family tree
> Deal with it, sister, that's just me

And while Lacey's maths homework had drifted down

 76

into the school pond, my voice stayed up. And got louder and better, as underneath me the instruments went from being separate into one proper sound. Into, I suppose, music.

I've got mad beats
I've got mad moves
I know your mum really disapproves

By the time I got to the second verse I'd stopped being embarrassed. In fact, I was hardly thinking at all.

If you're up for a laugh then you're my cup of tea
Friends forever, that's just me

Saying this is incredibly embarrassing, so I'll do it quickly and just get it over with, but as I was singing I really did feel as though I was growing stronger. I suppose it was a sense of togetherness with everyone, which is deeply bizarre as we were the least-together group that had ever existed on the face of the earth.

The end was pretty intense.

I've got mad love
I've got mad hate

Much bigger than it had been on the bus, too.

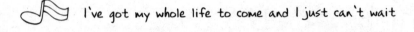 I've got my whole life to come and I just can't wait

Not just me, but everyone: Adrian thumping out his chords, Jaz whacking her drums, Lace giving it some on her tambourine, and Amanda doing a cool sort of flourish ...

And here's the thing, I think you'll agree
We're all in this together. It's not just me.

CHAPTER EIGHT

And then we were all laughing our heads off and Adrian was giving everyone high fives.

'That was excellent!'

'So cool!'

'I never knew you had such a good voice!'

It was exclamation-mark central.

'Oh, you know . . .' I said, trying to make the jump from worried hostess to lead singer.

'Did you get it all, Nicole?'

'I love that riff you did, right at the end . . .'

'Is anyone eating these chips or can I have them?'

The chips were stone cold and slimy and stuck together and soaking in fish grease. Even so, they were the most delicious thing anyone had ever eaten in the whole history of eating things.

'It sounded like a proper song,' said Lacey. 'You know, like the songs that you hear on the radio. It sounded like one of those.'

'I can't believe we made that noise.'

'I know.'

'I know!'

I swear to you, there was a glow in the room. Not the scary, radioactive one there'd been to start with, either. This glow was like the ones you get in make-up adverts. Everyone, and everything, right down to my dirty jeans pile, just seemed to shine.

In that moment, in fact, I could almost believe we *were* all in this together. That we were all on the same team, that the house wasn't so bad. That Adrian and Jaz weren't so bad, either, because how else could we have made that music?

Nicole and Lacey were doing this *boom boom, shake shake* thing between them, Mands was laughing and Adrian was saying:

'I wish Zoe had been home for this. She'd have been so proud of you both.'

I thought of just how much I'd have given for it to have been Dad with the keyboard on his lap, rather than Adrian – and the happy bubble exploded. Or, rather, imploded.

Anyway, it was gone.

'Mum's always proud of me,' I said. As I spoke it was

like the room snapped back into focus again. It was just me and a load of people who didn't really like each other. Plus a tube of skin cream and something that might once have been a pizza.

'Yeah, but if she'd just heard that—'

'Whatever,' I said, shooting the word full of ice. 'And Nicole, can you please stop filming everything? You're creeping me out.'

'Katie,' said Amanda, in her big-sister voice.

'I'm just saying,' I just said.

'What?'

'Nothing.'

'Sorry,' said Adrian. 'I didn't mean to . . . I don't understand . . .'

'No,' I said. 'Clearly you don't.'

He got to his feet, which took a while.

'You know, I think I'll leave you ladies to it.'

Thank the Lord he was off. But then Amanda jumped up too, and I really didn't want her to go. The atmosphere was already toxic, and that wasn't even including Nicole's body spray.

'You can stay if you want, Mands,' I said, with a hopeless smile.

But I'd left it too late.

'Ade and I are going to talk about restocking the shop.'

'Great OK fine,' I said. 'You two go and do that.'

'OK,' said Amanda, heading out the door. 'Have fun.'

'We will,' I said, as Nicole grabbed Lacey's bag and frisbee'd it out of the window.

'Ha ha ha,' said Jaz. By which I mean, she didn't laugh, she just said the words while looking Lacey straight in the eye.

'Yes, very funny,' said Lacey, also not laughing in the slightest. 'Are you going to go and get it then?'

At which point Nicole started climbing out of the window.

'No!' I said, rushing forward and pulling her down off the sill before she could actually kill herself. 'We're properly high up, you'll fall miles.'

'If anyone's going to fall out the window,' said Jaz, 'it should be Lacey.'

'What?!' Lacey's head snapped back round. 'Why?'

'Put you out of your misery.'

This was not looking good. I had to get Jaz to leave before something truly terrible happened. But how? Seeing as I hadn't actually invited her in the first place?

 82

Even with vampires, you have to ask them inside.

So while Jaz chucked Nicole chips, and Nicole tried and failed to catch them in her mouth, and Lacey pretended she was deeply interested in my Amy Winehouse memorabilia (which, from past experience, I knew she wasn't), I made a mental list of ways I might get Jaz to go away so I could talk to Lacey in peace.

- Say the evening is over and go to bed. (No. Jaz would probably set light to the duvet.)
- Fake a serious disease. (No. Nicole would probably catch it.)
- Have a huge fight and make Jaz storm out. (No. Jaz would win and I'd storm out and then I would be homeless and although the new house was not much fun it was better than a park bench.)
- Employ reverse psychology and tell Jaz that I want her to stay. (This could actually work. Nice one, me.)

I grinned and lay back against the wall, ultra-casual, trying not to notice that Nicole was pulling the shade off my bedside lamp. 'So, this has been a really fun evening.'

'Huh,' said Lacey.

'I'm so glad I'm getting the bus with you now,' I said to Jaz. 'It's brilliant.'

'It's all right,' said Jaz, but I could tell she was pleased.

'What's great about it, Jaz, is that we get to hang out a bit more,' I said. 'I feel like I've hardly seen you at school because of all the . . . all the . . .'

'Skiving?' said Lacey.

'And now we can do stuff. Which is why you should definitely stay a lot longer, if you want. Stay the night, even!'

I threw a quick glance at Lacey, with an expression that made it clear I was doing some very clever mind trickery that was going to get rid of Jaz pronto so we could enjoy some one-on-one friend time.

'If she's staying then I think I'm going to head off.'

'What?! No, Lace, you don't understand. I don't . . . I mean, I want you *all* to stay. *Especially* you.'

'I gave up seeing Gran's kitten to come over here. Because I thought we were going to watch *Mean Girls* together.' Lacey's skin was normally this soft milky colour, but now she'd flushed a bright and, I must say, quite unattractive shade of tomato.

'We can watch *Mean Girls*,' said Jaz.

'I thought *we* were going to watch *Mean Girls*,' said Lacey, blinking fast. 'To make up for not walking into school together.'

'And we will . . .'

'So how come you invited Mad Jaz – oh dear.'

'*Mad* Jaz?' said Mad Jaz.

'That's Katie's secret nickname for you,' said Lacey. 'It just slipped out. Whoops.'

'Why do you think I'm mad?' said Jaz, as I inwardly curled up into a tiny ball and rolled under the bed while I outwardly tried to look unbothered and respectful-of-Jaz.

'Just, you know.'

'No, I don't.'

'Oh dear, this is embarrassing,' said Lacey, looking the happiest she'd been all evening.

'It's j-just,' I stuttered, 'that you sometimes do things that are a bit . . . unexpected.'

'I love it. Mad Jaz! Best nickname ever. Thanks, Katie.'

'Maybe everyone should go home,' I said. 'Lace, it's not late, you could probably still see the kitten. And Jaz, you can . . . go and do . . . Jaz stuff.'

Amazingly, it worked. Everyone got up and started moving towards the door.

'Bye,' I said, shepherding them all down the stairs, which made ominous creaking noises as they went. 'Great seeing you. So much fun. Bye. Bye-bye!'

Then they were picking their way through the nettles in the front garden, and thank heaven it was almost over and I was just deciding to pretend that none of it had happened, when I had this sudden thought.

'Er, Jaz?' I called down the path. 'You won't post any of this online, will you?'

Jaz turned, and smiled, her teeth shining white through the dusk. 'I already have.'

CHAPTER NINE

At breakfast the next morning, there was a bit of an atmosphere. I know this because I was the one creating it.

'I see you had a party last night,' said Mum, looking meaningfully at the pile of fish-and-chip wrappers next to the kitchen bin. 'I hope you had a good time.'

'Not really,' I said.

'I had fun,' said Adrian. 'And your friend, Jaz? She's quite something.'

'I hate Jaz,' I said. Amanda raised her eyebrows. 'OK, not hate, but . . . she's not my friend, all right? She's just someone I know, who came over for the evening. That's all. And from now on can everyone please mind their own business.'

'What's upset her so much?' said Mum.

'You know Katie,' said Amanda, as though I wasn't sitting right there next to them. 'Drama queen. We're running out of Coco Pops. It's the world's greatest ever disaster.'

It was pretty disastrous, actually. But it wasn't why I

 87

was so upset. Although I have to say it didn't help.

What's the first thing you do when someone tells you they've put a video of you online?

You go and watch it.

Only I couldn't because my phone was dead. And the broadband, which had been the one thing that had been OK about the new house, suddenly seemed to have ceased to exist.

I'd given it an hour, and tried turning the box off and on and then off and then on. And smacking it against the wall, just in case. It was working, because the lights were on, but however much I refreshed the connection, our WiFi wouldn't come up.

I'd gone to bed with this itchy, crawly feeling that there was all this stuff out there and I couldn't see it. Not to mention all the other stuff I was missing. Devi Lester's latest conspiracy theory, whatever disgusting thing Nicole was up to, the pictures of Lacey's gran's kitten. It was like not being invited to a party. And as I literally hadn't been invited to Savannah's party, I wasn't feeling too great.

'Can someone *please* tell me why the broadband has stopped working?' I said.

'Oh. Yeah. That's switched off for the time being,' said Adrian, who was wearing his leather jacket at the breakfast table, the weirdo.

'What's the time being? Because I'm going to need it tonight.'

He creaked. Or his jacket did. 'The foreseeable future.'

'What?' My breathing went shallow. 'I cannot foresee a future without broadband.'

'Money's a bit tight at the moment. Takings are down; there are a few things wrong with the house that need to be fixed . . .'

'Like having no broadband.'

'It was either that or turn off the water, ha ha!'

I wasn't laughing. 'Then I'll go without water.'

'Adrian, why don't you go and unpack . . . something,' said Mum.

He shot out of the kitchen and, simultaneously, Mum and Amanda leaned in:

'How can you be so rude?'

'It's not his fault.'

Which was pushing it. 'He told us to buy the house, didn't he?'

'You should be nicer to him,' said Amanda.

 89

'You're right,' I replied. 'I should *jam* with him and maybe play all my private songs that I thought were just between the two of us.'

She flinched. 'I'm going to help Adrian unpack . . . some . . . thing.'

Now it was me and Mum and a table's worth of breakfast dishes.

I wouldn't say anything else, I decided. Not while I was so worked up. I'd only talk my way into trouble.

Unfortunately, Mum has got this killer technique for getting me to open up. I think she learned it at nursing college. It involves kneeling down and brushing the hair out of my eyes and saying, 'Katie, love, what is it? Are you OK? Because I'm worried about you.'

I lasted all of nine seconds.

'It's just, the house.'

Wrong answer. She stood back up again.

'We're all upset about the house,' said Mum.

'And, I suppose, Adrian.'

'What about Adrian?' asked Mum, swinging round to the sink.

'Um.'

'Do you have a problem with Adrian?' Now she was doing

90

some really intense washing-up. The sort of washing-up that made it clear she didn't want to hear the answer.

'No,' I said.

A big, long gap.

Don't say it, I thought. It won't help.

Scrub scrub, splish splish.

'It's just . . . I thought you weren't going to go out with another musician. Because of Dad, and everything. You kept saying it, all through the break-up. And now—'

'Adrian is *not* a musician,' said Mum, and she said it very fast and very sharp. 'He's in retail.'

'He was in a band, though.'

'That was then.'

'Still, he's always noodling about on the guitar, isn't he? Him and Amanda—'

'I think Amanda's been terrific recently,' said Mum. 'Very calm, very supportive.' I was clearly being invited to consider another member of the family who hadn't been quite so angelic.

'Yeah,' I said. It was becoming obvious that Mum didn't want to know *why* I'd been such a grump. She just wanted the grumping to stop.

'And what's the big upset about the broadband?

 91

Why can't you use your phone?'

'Ah,' I said. 'About that. It's sort of . . . broken.'

Mum did that thing she does when she is Being Calm in the Face of Adversity. The current adversity being me. 'You broke your birthday present?'

'I didn't break it, OK? This boy on the bus chucked it out of the window.'

'I suppose I thought you'd take better care of it. That phone was incredibly expensive.'

She wasn't hearing anything I said.

'If I hadn't had to catch the bus in the first place, this wouldn't have happened,' I said. 'It's not *my* fault we had to move house.'

'Katie, I have a headache coming on and you're not helping.'

'Well, I'm sorry I'm such a pain,' I said. 'And I guarantee that from now on you will hardly notice my existence. It'll be like I've disappeared.'

'Katie . . .'

'You won't even notice I'm around. Then, one day, you'll find the Coco Pops packet is empty and you'll be all, like, "Oh yes, my other daughter," and –'

Mum took off her rubber gloves and stood back in

 92

a way that told me this conversation was over. 'Katie, knock it off.'

Which made me completely livid, because she'd started out like she cared and really she'd just wanted to have a go at me.

What with all that, I wasn't really up for lingering around at home, and I got to the bus stop even earlier than I had the day before.

No one should ever have to wait for a bus without a phone. It's unnatural. I mean, what are your hands supposed to even do? Why do humans have thumbs, if not for messaging?

And then I got distracted from my scientific considerations because Finlay had arrived and he was staring at me.

I tried a bit of a smile on him, to show that I'd forgiven him for destroying my beloved mobile. Which I hadn't. I just couldn't face him destroying anything else.

He just smirked and said, 'You're really messy.'

'I am quite messy, yes,' I said, because I suppose I am.

Then he smirked. So I decided he was an idiot and left him to it while I dealt with the year sevens, who all arrived at once, singing the chorus of 'Just Me'.

They had the words and tune down perfectly, which was pretty impressive, given that they'd only heard it that one time on the bus. And they sang it over and over and over and over and over again.

'That's great, thanks,' I said, thinking it would shut them up. Instead it seemed to put them into overdrive.

'All right, maybe you can stop now,' I tried, which of course made it infinitely worse.

Then Nicole turned up. I wanted to ask her about the video, and whether I could watch it, only before I could, she started telling me a long story about her BCG scab, which ended with her picking it off and eating it.

'Maybe we could talk about something else . . . ?'

'Maybe you could do some washing,' said one of the year sevens, and then they all sniggered.

Honestly. In my day we showed our elders a bit of respect.

I spent the entire bus ride trying to keep Finlay from shoving tuna mayo down the back of my neck, while Nicole seared the word 'Nicole' into the seats with a compass and her lighter.

What with having to make a quick trip to the loos to

de-fish myself, I only just made it to registration, and as I sat down everyone giggled.

'What?' I said, just as McAllister came in and said, 'Assembly. All of you. Now.'

Assembly that day was a lecture on plants – how we are all like plants and should grow towards the light and something about chlorophyll.

I'm a little hazy on that last part because I'd only been listening, vaguely, probably picking my nose or drooling or feeling around in one of my back teeth for trapped Coco Pops or something similarly embarrassing, when I started to notice that things were slightly . . . off.

Like how you don't realize for a little while that you're running a temperature, and instead find the world has gone a bit funny? Well, I could feel the weight of a thing happening. As though I was heating up, only I wasn't, or like I'd accidentally sat under a hand-dryer, which I hadn't.

My eyes slid from the stage, down to my lap and across to the next row. A load of jumbled-up arms and legs, frayed bits of uniform, a few things that definitely weren't uniform, a smell of feet and farts and . . .

Eyes. Eyes everywhere, and all of them looking at me.

The heat that I'd been feeling was the collective gaze

of nine hundred and fifty people. Nineteen hundred individual eyes, although really I should say eighteen hundred and ninety-nine because there's a poor girl in the year above us who has to wear a patch.

The Head finished her speech and we all stood up. Now, we're not allowed to talk in assembly, and on the way in, people are pretty good about it. On the way out, though, everyone's in a hurry, the teachers are distracted, and everything's a bit more chatty.

Which is when I heard snatches of 'Just Me'.

Not just from the bus crew.

Not even just from my form.

But from every corner of the hall.

And it just didn't make sense. No one knew about that song except for me, and Lace and Mands and Adrian. And Nicole and Jaz and Jaz's phone . . .

Oh God.

Oh GOD.

The year sevens, singing on the bus . . .

Finlay, calling me messy . . .

The whole entire assembly hall . . .

OHGODOHGODOHGOD

According to the clock I had eight minutes until the

start of Maths. So I tore through the crowds and up the stairs into the tech lab, logging in with shaking fingers, then hammering my name into Google. And there was the video. Jaz had tagged it 'Katie Cox sings Just Me Quirky Kooky Feisty SO REAL' and there'd been seven hundred and fifty-seven views and it was . . .

Blocked.

Stupid school computer!

I tried again and it came up and just as quickly went away.

But it was there . . . it was definitely there . . .

And everyone had seen it.

I raced back down the stairs and there was Dominic Preston by the lockers, watching me with his gorgeous eyes – eyes that must have seen the video because then he actually smiled at me.

Aaaaaargh!

And into the form room, and I was panting now and I didn't even care because there was Savannah with her gold-plated phone.

'Can I please borrow that?' I said, making a grab for it.

She gave me a Savannah look, one of the particularly withering ones, and said, 'Er, you do not

 97

touch my phone, thanks, babes.'

'But, the video . . .' I said.

'It's my phone,' said Savannah. 'Get off.'

I went in for another swipe. 'Please?!'

'DO NOT TOUCH MY PHONE,' said Savannah, with Paige and Sofie sliding in on either side of her as backup.

I took a few deep breaths.

'Savannah, I don't want to touch your phone, I promise. I just want to watch the video, because I haven't seen it. Apparently I'm the only one.'

She rolled her eyes, and then, amazingly, she unlocked it and let me lean in.

There I was, singing away, everyone else playing in the background, while in real life Savannah hovered beside me in her non-regulation heels, smelling of Gucci eau de toilette.

I looked at the screen, trying to make sense of it. Something odd was going on. Perhaps my eyes had gone funny. Or maybe the shock of it all had given me brain damage.

Because just a few minutes ago there'd definitely been seven hundred and fifty-seven views.

Now, there were ten and a half thousand.

CHAPTER TEN

I thought I might pass out. Everything went hot and cold and then hot and a bit swirly for good measure.

'Ten and a half thousand,' I said. 'Ten and a half thousand. Ten and a half thousand.'

Voices, far away.

'Why does she keep saying "ten and a half thousand"?'

'Maybe she's ill.'

'She looks ill.'

'No, that's just her face.'

'Katie? Katie!'

'Put your head between your knees . . .'

'Er, can I have my phone back first? OMG. Paige. She has eleven thousand hits.'

'Maybe that's why she's passing out. Katie!'

I opened my eyes to see Savannah's face entirely filling my vision. Interestingly, her cheeks had this microscopic coating of white fuzzy down on them, like a peach. I examined the fuzz for a while, until I noticed that her mouth was moving.

 99

'Babes. Babes! You need to focus. You have eleven –' she glanced down at her phone – '*fourteen* thousand hits. Also, you need to go to Maths.'

My legs somehow began working again and lifted me up and into an approximation of a normal person.

'Fourteen thousand?'

'It's going up again,' said Sofie. And Savannah said:

'Can people *please* stop touching my phone.'

I made my way over to Maths and the world seemed to be crackling with electricity. Walking through the corridor, up the stairs, all I could think was – who were all these people?

And why were they listening to me?

I plunked down into my seat next to Lacey. Thank goodness for my best friend! Whatever craziness was going on in my life right now, she would rescue me. I wouldn't be facing it alone.

'I cannot believe this is happening,' said Lacey.

'I know,' I said.

'Everyone in the school has seen it. Like, everyone.'

'And—'

'*Everyone*,' said Lacey.

'I know, I just saw. Fourteen thousand people! Probably more by now. I don't think I can even imagine what that looks like!' I had a quick go. 'Nope. I can't.'

'Fourteen THOUSAND?' said Lacey. 'This is crazy, Katie. This is bananas.'

'Isn't it?' I laughed, semi-hysterically.

'Why are you laughing?'

'I don't know!'

'When you've made me look so stupid!'

Hang on, what?

I thought back to my bedroom floor, and my blackhead cream and my school uniform, and the boxes and the way my eyes closed when I sang the hard parts and the fish-and-chip wrappers and I said:

'*I've* made *you* look stupid?'

'People keep telling me to cheer up. And asking me what I've done with my tambourine.'

'It's Adrian's tambourine.'

'KATIE!'

'What? I'm just saying.'

In films, you have major dramas on the tops of buildings, or cliffs, or jumping between spaceships. Not in Maths.

 101

'You have to take it down.'

'I didn't put it up! Jaz did! Lace, I'm as embarrassed about it as you are!'

'Are you?'

'Of course I am! It wasn't like I planned for this to happen.'

'I never gave you my permission. I know you sound nice and it's catchy and everything, but I'm not going to be a part of this.'

'I'm sure it'll fizzle out soon enough,' I said. 'I mean, that's what happens with these things, isn't it? They come, they go, they—'

'Good morning, everyone.' Miss Allen swept in, all big jewellery and scarves. 'Katie, stop talking. Now.'

'I'll ask Jaz,' I whispered, when Allen had finished telling me off. 'I'll get her to take it down.'

'Promise?'

'Promise.'

But it wasn't that simple tracking Jaz down, what with her not behaving like any kind of normal person. I'd have to investigate places I'd never been to before, really get into the underbelly of the school, all the dark corners I'd never normally visit.

Or, I could get Nicole to text her, which is what I did.

And it turned out she wasn't in school at all. She was spending a day in town.

Which worked for me, as my need for a new phone had gone from dire to extra super extremely desperate. All those zillions of people, watching me, and I couldn't even get online . . .

They could use it as a form of torture. I reckon it would break anyone. Even James Bond.

After the slowest, strangest day in the history of time, where every classroom echoed with snatches of 'Just Me' and even the teachers were looking at me funny, I finally got myself to the high street.

According to the Tourist Information leaflets, Harltree high street is one of the two main attractions of Harltree. The second one is the station, and I'm not completely sure that counts as a Harltree attraction, because if you're going there it's because you're trying to leave.

I looked up and down, my Mad Jaz radar on full alert. The usual suspects were out in force: mothers and their tank-sized buggies, some kid screaming over a dropped ice cream, a group of scary-looking blokes and their scary-looking dog. And . . .

'Katie!'

She was standing right next to me.

'Hey, Jaz. I was just looking for you!'

'Want some body lotion?' Jaz opened her bag and showed me about ten bottles. 'I've just been to Superdrug.'

'Why did you buy so much body lotion? Oh, you didn't buy it. I see. No thanks, I mean, it's kind of you to offer, but I'm OK for lotion just now.' I walked her around the corner in case a security guard was about to come running out and throw us into prison for the next hundred years. 'Um, about the video.'

'I know. Have you seen?'

'Not recently,' I said. 'On account of Finlay breaking my phone. I was just on my way to get another one.'

'Great,' said Jaz, striding off towards the phone shop. 'I need some new headphones.'

Trying not to think about whether Jaz was planning on paying for the headphones, I followed her inside. The sales assistants were all busy, mostly talking to each other, so I went and stood as far from audio accessories as possible.

'Here's the thing about the video,' I began. 'You need to take it down.'

'Why?'

'It's really embarrassing.'

'Is it?'

'Yes!' I said. 'I know you put it up for a laugh and everything but . . .'

Jaz was contemplating an iPad, which, thankfully, was bolted to the wall. 'I thought you liked writing songs.'

'I do.'

'And you sang at everyone on the bus.'

'But this is different.'

'Is it?' said Jaz. 'Or is it the same, but better?'

I decided to try something different. 'Look, Jaz, everyone's seen it now.'

'If everyone's seen it,' said Jaz, 'then why take it down?'

I didn't have a good answer, which was a shame.

'And anyway,' said Jaz. 'Not *everyone* has seen it. Two hundred thousand, seven hundred and twenty-one people have seen it. That still leaves the rest of the world which hasn't.'

'Two hundred thousand?'

'You're smiling,' said Jaz.

'I'm in shock.'

'You're pleased,' said Jaz.

She was looking at me, hard, and I thought all over again how strange it is that someone can be making a complete mess of their life and yet still be incredibly clever. Jaz could see exactly what I was thinking even before I'd quite realized it myself, and yet she hadn't noticed that she was a disaster area who terrified everyone around her and was probably about to get expelled.

'For the record, I am not pleased. I am horrified. And humiliated.' I picked at the loose skin around my thumb. 'Sorry, did you really say *two hundred thousand*?'

'Last time I checked. It's probably gone up since then.'

'When did you check?'

'I don't know. Maybe half an hour ago?'

'So it probably *has* gone up . . .'

'Can I help you?'

A bored-looking bloke came ambling across the shop. He didn't look like he wanted to help me. He didn't look like he wanted to help anyone.

'Er, yes. My phone's broken. I need a replacement.' I gave him my name and address.

He scrolled up and down on his computer until he

 106

found it. 'Got you. Replacement handset, yes?'

'Yes please.' From the corner of my eye I could see Jaz doing something awful to a rack of leaflets.

'A hundred and eighty.' He said it in this bored way, clearly not noticing that his words meant misery and doom.

'Pounds?'

'Yeah.'

Cold sweat came prickling out from wherever cold sweat comes from. 'I haven't got a hundred and eighty pounds. I've got fifteen pounds.' I mentally added on my emergency tenner and a few days' worth of lunch money. Lacey would share her sandwiches. 'Maybe forty. At most.'

'Then you can have this,' said the bloke, and he pulled out the worst, the most useless, the brick-iest phone anyone has ever seen.

'Does it have internet?'

'Nope.'

'Apps?'

'You can use it to make calls,' said Mr I Really Don't Care. 'And text. Oh, and we're giving away a free Karamel single download with every purchase. But you won't be able to play it on that.'

'OK,' I said, cursing inside that I wasn't old enough to have a job and earn money and instead had to depend on Christmas and birthday presents to meet my technology requirements. 'Thank you.' And I went to the till and handed over my cash.

Jaz was waiting by the door. 'Got it?'

'Yeah, but it's pretty much useless.' I showed her the box. 'Did you check? How many?'

'Three hundred and forty thousand, two hundred and thirty-three. This could change your life. You could . . .' Jaz stopped walking for a second, clearly trying to think of some things that could happen. 'You could get a decent phone.'

I wouldn't normally go to Jaz to predict the future. But I did begin to think that maybe she might just have a point. Maybe, somehow, this *could* change my life. I wasn't quite sure how, but . . .

'If you want me to take it down, I will,' said Jaz. She had her phone out, her thumb hovering over the screen. 'I can do it right now.'

For a moment, I hesitated.

Because I had promised Lacey.

Because having the whole entire world look into

108

my bedroom was super spooky. No, scratch that. The bedroom thing wasn't nearly as weird as the fact that I'd sort of shown the whole entire world the contents of my head.

Only, in another way, wasn't it sort of great that they'd seen it? That they were watching because they liked it . . . ?

And then, all at once, I knew I just couldn't ask Jaz to take it down, not when this was by a million miles the most exciting thing that had ever happened to me.

'Maybe leave it,' I said, trying to sound casual. 'For now. Might as well see how far it goes!'

'All right,' said Jaz, swinging off towards the bus station, her bag hanging heavy and low with body lotion and goodness knows what else.

I'd just tell Lacey that Jaz had refused. It was believable enough.

And it wouldn't be a lie, exactly – or at least, only a very small one.

It was, I told my stomach, definitely the right decision.

Song for a Broken Phone

I loved your camera
I loved your apps
I loved your GPS and your maps

I loved your screen
I loved your charger
I loved the way you made pictures larger

But your screen is smashed
And your case is broken
Messages gone
Voicemail unspoken

He threw it as a joke
But it wasn't very funny
And I can't upgrade you
Cos I haven't got the money.

CHAPTER ELEVEN

Adrian came home that night as happy as anything, with a great big bag of ham and pineapple pizzas.

'Reduced! Love a bit of pineapple on my pizza.'

And then he started asking Mum about her day while simultaneously nibbling at her earlobe.

'Mainly,' said Mum, who, for once, seemed to be finding Adrian's attentions as annoying as I did, 'I spent the day talking to people who'd come to tell me they'd seen you all on the internet. Perhaps next time you could tell me *before* you decide to become famous?'

I sat up a bit straighter. 'You saw it! What did you think?'

'Whoah there, horsey,' said Adrian, before Mum could tell me how proud she was and how lovely I'd sounded and stuff like that. 'We're online?'

'Jaz put it up,' I told him. 'I didn't ask her to but she did. And it's doing quite well.'

'Nice one,' said Adrian.

'Well . . .'

 111

As I spoke I found that I hadn't considered how I'd tell them all. And that half of me wanted to pretend that it wasn't a particularly big deal, that stuff like this happened to me all the time, that Adrian's stupid jamming session hadn't been an event or anything and that I was basically totally chilled about it.

That half of me was almost immediately overwhelmed by the other half, which was hugely excited and couldn't keep its mouth shut.

'Actually, it's better than that,' I said. 'I've – we've – it's gone really big. Thousands of people have watched it. Hundreds of thousands.'

'What the –'

Mum stood up just as Amanda spilt her squash all over the table, which Adrian was giving a thump. 'Katie, this is huge.'

And Amanda said, 'Why didn't you tell me?'

'Because you were at work,' I said. 'And anyway, it doesn't mean anything.'

'*Of course* it means something,' said Amanda. 'Of course it does!'

'Can I see it?' said Adrian.

Mands had her phone out.

'There,' I said. 'Over four hundred thousand views!'

'That's nearly half a million people,' said Mum, and I saw that she was shaking.

We all huddled around the screen, and for a second I thought about how in the olden days everyone used to huddle around the fireplace and then I gave up on my historical musings because there I was on the video, singing, and that was much more interesting.

Without a load of people talking and clattering up and down the corridor, I could hear the sound properly, and all the words. And yeah, it was sort of amateurish and there were bits where we weren't quite together but in a way it made it better. It gave it credibility.

'That girl's got a face like a wet weekend,' said Mum. 'Oh hang on, that's Lacey.'

'She *was* in a bit of a strop,' I said.

'And who's that on the drums? In all the black floppy stuff? She looks like a bat.'

'Mad Jaz.'

'And that's you, Amanda?' said Mum. Honestly, she was looking at everyone except me.

'That's my foot,' said Amanda, looking at me rather sourly, even though it wasn't my fault she'd been cut off.

Nicole was the one holding the phone, not me.

The onscreen Katie was just getting into *I'm the big bad apple on the family tree* and for once, it sounded as good as it had in my head.

'We weren't quite together there, were we?' said Adrian. 'You came in a bit quicker than we were expecting, Katie.'

'I dropped a beat,' said Amanda.

'That's Katie's timing,' said Adrian. Then, to me, 'Don't worry. We can work on that.'

'Oh, can we?'

'Absolutely. That and your breath control. See how you run out of air on the ends of lines?'

'That was on purpose.'

'You need to be thinking about your diaphragm. Breathe from your stomach, not your chest. Then there's your diction. If you're going to sell the song then you need to be thinking about—'

And just like that, I'd had enough. 'You know what? Why can't you just say you like it?'

'We do like it,' said Mum.

'Instead of being all "Katie this" and "Katie that" and "Katie you can't breathe" and "Katie your timing's off", why can't you just say well done?'

'Constructive criticism,' said Adrian. 'No one's perfect.'

'Four hundred thousand people seem to like it,' I said. 'Four hundred thousand people seem to think my breathing is excellent.'

'You have to remember that Adrian was in a band,' said Amanda. 'He knows what he's talking about.'

'Maybe we should be listening to his stuff, then,' I said. 'Maybe we should turn off your phone and spend the rest of the evening enjoying Adrian's clear diction and excellent timing.'

Which I meant sarcastically.

So you can imagine how I felt when that is exactly what we did.

Adrian's band was called Vox Popular and, as he told us, a lot, 'it was in that lull between eighties synth and Britpop. Like an electro Blur, but pre-Blur.'

Not my kind of thing at all.

I turned the record over and there were two blokes on the sleeve. One had dark hair and a stonewashed denim jacket and eyes that were sort of sleepy. And the other one was Adrian, about a million years younger, with all this hair on his head, wearing a leather jacket, but a much smaller one, cut tight around the top of his jeans. I caught myself, for about a microsecond, thinking that he'd been quite good-looking.

Yikes. Katie, you need to wash your brain out with soap and water. And maybe some fire, just to be on the safe side.

'You can really play,' said Amanda, the big suck-up.

'And you can *really* sing,' said Mum, in a way that made me cringe so hard I was genuinely in danger of bursting a kidney.

'Well,' said Adrian, lifting up the needle so we could listen to it all over again, 'I dunno about that. God, I haven't played this in years.'

Interesting then, I thought, that in a house of complete chaos, he knew exactly where to find it. It was suspiciously undusty, too.

I noticed there was a bit of a silence. Clearly I was supposed to say something pleasant.

'How many did you sell?' I asked.

'All together?'

'All together.'

He fiddled with an invisible bit of something off the table. 'We . . . we didn't. We cut the single, but before it came out, we split up. Creative differences.'

'So you didn't sell one? Not a single single?'

'Never had the chance,' said Adrian.

'And I've had four hundred thousand people listen to my song.'

'Katie!'

'I'm just saying.'

Mum and Amanda both started talking at once, presumably in some kind of race to see who could tell me to shut up first, but before they could, Adrian waved a meaty hand.

'She's right, she's right. Tell you what, K, want me to put in a call to Tony?' He pointed down at Sleepy Eyes. 'He's still in the industry, got his own label now. Top Music.'

That Adrian knew anyone in the music business was doubtful. That the dude in the denim had his own label was incredibly unlikely. And that this man would have any interest in me seemed beyond impossible.

I opened my mouth, but Mum was ahead of me.

'Absolutely not.'

'But—'

'Katie is not going to follow in her father's footsteps,'

said my mother, and I hadn't seen her so upset in a long time. 'I don't mind this as a . . . hobby. But that's all.'

'It's just a video,' I said.

'And that's fine. That's terrific. But you're not to go getting ideas.'

If someone tells you not to get ideas, it's a guaranteed way to start getting ideas. Really. They should stick it at the top of our creative writing paper in English.

'But if Adrian can—'

'Nope,' said Mum.

'Can we at least watch it again?' I asked.

And so we did.

CHAPTER TWELVE

'Lacey.'

It was first break, which I always think is a really bad name for what is basically a massive dash to hit the loo, the vending machine and the lockers all in fifteen minutes. Hardly a break. Even netball is more relaxing.

'Lacey!'

'WHAT?'

'I just thought we ought to have a talk. About everything.'

She folded her arms. 'OK. Let's have a talk.'

The sight of Lacey standing there with a white face and a stance that can only be described as 'confrontational' gave me complete conversation paralysis. Even her elbows were giving me evils.

'Um,' I said.

'Last night we went to get petrol,' said Lacey, 'and the bloke behind the counter was singing it. And when he saw me he started waving this stupid imaginary tambourine.'

'At the petrol station?' I said, trying to decide whether

119

I was pleased at the idea that now completely random people were watching. 'Which one?'

'I don't know!' said Lacey, her elbows angrier than ever.

'The one on the main road? The one by Sainsbury's? Or that one up past the church, or the one by the chip shop—'

'Stop listing petrol stations!'

'Sorry. I just want to know what he said.'

'That his little sister has listened to it a hundred times and now they can't stop singing it even though it's really annoying.' She said that last part with a relish that I found inappropriate.

'That's great,' I replied.

'I'm glad you think so.'

'And then Auntie Rachel phoned from Scotland because she'd seen me in it and told Mum that my fringe looked bad.'

'Your fringe looks great! It really brings out your eyes.'

She smiled slightly. 'Do you think so? You need to get one. I've got scissors, somewhere . . .' She started rootling through her bag. So I jumped in before anything terrible could happen.

'Isn't this a tiny bit amazing, though? That people in Scotland are watching? I mean, I know it's embarrassing that strangers are doing tambourines at you, but isn't it sort of awesome, too?'

Judging from the way that Lacey's expression changed, I should probably have just let her chop me a fringe right then and there. In fact, I should probably have let her shave my entire head.

'Why is it still up?' said Lacey. 'You said Jaz was going to take it down. Why hasn't she?'

'I asked her to,' I said, hoping Lace wouldn't notice that my left eyelid had started to twitch. Besides, I *had* asked her. It wasn't a complete lie, so long as you ignored the conversation afterwards. 'I asked and then I begged and she just laughed. You know what Jaz is like.'

'Ask her again.'

'I will. But . . . I sort of worry that the more we ask her to take it down, the longer she'll keep it up there.'

Lacey sighed. 'Yeah. There is that, I suppose. Kit Kat?' She snapped off a finger and waved it at me.

'Ta.'

Thank the Lord we were finally having a proper conversation. Because it hurts, having your best friend

 121

turn on you. It's like being attacked by your pillow or something.

'I'm sorry it's so embarrassing for you, though,' I said.

'Aren't you embarrassed?'

'My bedroom is in a bit of a state, isn't it?' I admitted. 'And I wish I'd worn more make-up.'

'Yeah,' Lacey agreed. 'You do look pretty awful.'

'Huh.'

'And that thing you do with your nostrils on the high notes is so bizarre!'

'Um.'

'It's like your whole face goes into this *spasm* . . .'

'Er.'

'It's a good thing you sound nice. They were playing it on the *Breakfast Show* this morning and—'

I grabbed her by the shoulders. 'Seriously? That's huge.'

'Yeah,' said Lacey sadly. 'A load more people to laugh at me.'

'Lacey,' I said, trying to be casual, 'can I look at it on your phone? Just for a sec?'

She fished it out of her pocket, still talking about how the guy at the petrol station had been asking where he could buy the single and how should she know, and then, as I was about to check in on my numbers –

'I'll have that, thank you, Lacey.' McAllister materialized in front of us. 'No phones in the corridors.'

'But—'

'And Katie, I have a message for you from the Head. She wants you in her office, now.'

'But—'

'Now,' said McAllister.

I turned up at the school reception and hung around by all the glossy posters. These had quite impressed Mum the first time she came in, until me and Mands explained that they're only glossy so you can peel the chewing gum off them without causing any damage. They didn't laminate the first set and I think they lasted about a day and a half.

So I pretended to admire a poster about how many different types of vegetable you can get in our canteen (a very exciting four) until the school secretary looked up and saw me, and shook her head in a sort of general disapproval at my existence, following it up with:

'Wait here, please. There's something of a queue today.'

At which point I looked across at the sofa to see the queue, which consisted of Mad Jaz.

'What are you doing here?' I whispered.

'The usual,' said Jaz, who apparently had a usual. 'You?'

'I don't even know,' I said. Then, because I was clearly in enough trouble that it didn't matter if I got into more, and the itch to find out how the video was doing was unbearable, 'Can I borrow your phone?'

She dropped it into my lap and I brought up the video. Eight hundred and eighty thousand, two hundred and sixty-six views.

'I know,' said Jaz, hearing me sigh. 'You really need to start turning this into money.'

'Katie?' It was the secretary. 'If you'd like to go through . . .'

Believe me when I say that I'm not a regular in the Head's office. The very few times I'd been in before were owing to extreme misunderstandings and were in no way a reflection of my personality, which is to never break the rules unless absolutely necessary.

'Now, Katie.' The Head was watching me intently, as

though she was seeing all this other stuff instead of just my face.

I tried to look innocent. And academically minded.

'I've had some calls. Quite a few calls. About this video.'

'I'm sorry,' I said.

'Don't be. You're not in trouble.'

'Aren't I?'

'A number of journalists want to speak to you.'

'What, like, from the *Harltree Gazette*?'

'One of them was from the *Harltree Gazette*, yes. And one of them was –' the Head cleared her throat, this delicate little 'ahem' – 'from the BBC.'

My knees started to shake, and I had to sit down in one of the Head's special chairs.

'Now, you don't have to if you don't want to, but we just wondered, if you *did* want to speak to them, whether doing so here might be . . . fun? We could set you up with a little table. In front of the trophy cabinet.'

'Won't we have to win some trophies?' I said. 'Because that might take a while. Especially the way the netball team's been playing lately.'

'We, er, we do have some backups that we could

put in there,' said the Head. 'Mr Griffin has just made an emergency visit to the engravers.' She twiddled a pen. 'You don't have to, of course. But if you did want to mention our music programme and the exemplary teaching you've received here . . .'

Hang on, was the Head asking *me* for a favour?

'If you like,' I said.

She looked very, very happy. 'You'll be in school uniform, of course.' She peered at me. 'Maybe not that particular version of school uniform. We'll find you something ironed. If you can just wait a few minutes, I'll let them know.'

'Wait, let who know?'

The Head raised her blind, slat by dusty slat.

A row of cars, big ones, were parked along the *No Parking* bit at the front of the school. And there was a van, with satellite dishes on its roof.

'I'll tell them half an hour, shall I?' said the Head. She must have caught a whiff of my panic. 'Go and get yourself a glass of water. And tell Jasmine she can come back at the same time tomorrow.'

I escaped back into the lobby to find Jaz picking holes in her seat and pulling out the lining. She'd got about four fluffy caterpillars' worth and had them lined up next to her.

'You've been let off for twenty-four hours,' I told her.

'Why?'

'Because I've got . . . This is so . . . Because I'm about to have a press conference. Jaz, what will I say? And what do I even look like? I haven't got my make-up with me!'

A smile spread across Jaz's face.

'Let me help you with that,' she said.

CHAPTER THIRTEEN

'Right, here we go,' said the Head, in full-on bustle mode. 'Come this way – oh. Oh my goodness.'

'Is it all right?' I said. 'I was thinking that I ought to make a bit of an effort, if people are going to see me.'

'It's . . . your choice I suppose,' said the Head, handing me a fresh sweatshirt, still with its tags on.

It's worth saying here that the Head wears no make-up whatsoever. Which, I thought to myself, was the only way to explain her very extreme reaction to Jaz having given me the tiniest bit of eyeliner.

'They're all very nice,' said the Head. 'And I'll be next to you.' She guided me down the staff corridor and into the admin room. 'Don't forget our music programme. You've found it very helpful.'

She opened the door on to a scene of complete mayhem.

On the one hand, it was just the admin room. So, even though someone had made a bit of an effort, with a school banner and a nice arrangement of desks and a suspiciously full trophy cabinet, it was still just a stuffy corner of the school that smelt of teachers' coffee.

On the other hand, it was this kind of portal to Weird World. Because it was absolutely full. On one side were all my teachers.

And on the other side were a load of people I'd never seen before in my life.

'One at a time,' said the Head. 'If you're ready, Katie.'

'Not really,' I said, and they all laughed, as though I'd made a hilarious joke. I noticed several cameras, pointing straight at me.

'Becky Haddon, BBC *Look East*. How does it feel to have over nine hundred thousand hits?'

'I . . . I don't know,' I said.

There was this awkward silence. It occurred to me that perhaps this wasn't the answer they'd been hoping for.

'OK. It feels like . . . ' I thought for a second. 'You know those dreams, where you're standing in a very, very, very small room and you feel like you're kind of safe, I suppose it's probably a womb thing, that's what my mate Lacey says, her mum's really into all that stuff. So you're in the room and you're feeling kind of held and snug and then one by one the walls drop away and you're actually standing on top of a mountain with the wind whipping around you. And when you look down, instead of the usual mountain stuff, like trees or snow or . . . goats . . . it's like, just people, all watching, and then you realize you've got no clothes on. It's sort of like that.'

Big silence.

'But in a good way,' I added.

'Katie loves our music programme,' said the Head. 'She's found it very helpful.'

'Mm,' I said. 'Very.'

'Alex Hayward-Bradley, the *Harltree Gazette*. Tell us about your influences?'

'I've got this major thing for Amy Winehouse,' I told him. This was easier than I'd thought. 'Then there's Lily Allen, remember her? And for pure pop, anything by Cathy Dennis. I've recently been in a bit of a country groove, which started with early Taylor Swift and then got completely out of control, and now it's all about Dolly Parton, Emmylou Harris and breakthroughs like Caitlin Rose.'

'Katie has been very influenced by our music programme,' said the Head.

'I have,' I agreed.

'And what's next for you, Katie?'

I had to have a bit of a think about this one. 'Geography.'

When I finally got out it was lunchtime. A minute ago I'd been feeling quite sick, but one sniff of the canteen and I found myself really fancying some shepherd's pie.

'Katie!' Sofie was waving at me, so I took my plate and joined her.

'Hello,' I said.

'Is it really true that you just did a press conference?' she asked.

'Yup.'

'What did you say?'

I thought back to what I had said.

'Just . . . stuff.'

'And you did it looking like that!' said Sofie.

'The Head gave me a new sweatshirt,' I said, and then saw I'd already got pie down it.

'No, your face,' said Sofie.

'What about my face?'

Then Paige appeared and shouted, 'YOUR FACE! KATIE, WHAT HAPPENED?'

I felt it over with my fingers. Everything still seemed

to be there. A nose, two eyes . . .

'She's making it worse,' said Paige. 'Katie, stop smudging it.'

'Smudging what? Will someone please give me a mirror?'

Someone gave me a mirror, which made me immediately regret having asked for a mirror.

It also made me regret giving Jaz a liquid eyeliner pen and full, unsupervised access to my face.

'It's like you've got spiders instead of eyes,' said Paige.

'It's like you put your make-up on in a car,' said Sofie.

'A dodgem car,' said Paige.

'I cannot believe I did a press conference looking like this,' I screamed, at which point the whole table laughed so loudly that we got a telling-off from the dinner lady.

'I cannot believe you are having the shepherd's pie,' said Savannah, joining us with her plate. 'It's cruelty plus calories. You have to go vegetarian, Katie; it's the only feasible option.'

'But you're eating a burger,' I said.

'Yes,' said Savannah, as though she was explaining something to a particularly idiotic child. 'But it's a chicken burger.'

'Chicken is meat,' I said.

'Er, no,' said Savannah. 'I mean, yes, it might be meat in the scientific sense, but it's not meaty-type meat.'

'She's right,' said Sofie. 'It's not.'

I'd never eaten lunch with Savannah and co. before. And it was kind of interesting, being this close to the action. Even if the action was currently picking the bread off its plate and saying, 'I'm not feeling the carbs today.'

'Katie had a press conference,' said Sofie. 'That's why there were all those vans outside.'

Savannah's blue eyes slid into focus and, suddenly, I knew how it felt to be a chicken burger.

'Did you?'

I nodded.

'Katie,' said Savannah. 'I have been thinking. A lot. About you going viral, and my party. And how one affects the other.'

I waited.

'There's this thing called the butterfly effect,' said Savannah. 'How, if a butterfly flaps its wings in Japan, there's an earthquake in New York.'

'Right.'

'And I was thinking that our situation is a bit like that.

 133

Only you're the butterfly and your video is the flapping and I am New York. Mmm?'

'I'm sorry,' I said. 'I'm having trouble following you.'

'What I'm saying is, would you like to come to my party?'

'Oh!' This was big. 'Yes please! Thank you!' *Don't sound so grateful, Katie.* 'I mean, if I'm free.' *Don't sound so ungrateful, Katie.* 'Which I will be.'

'We should go shopping for something to wear,' said Sofie.

'You do not want to shop with Sofie,' said Paige. 'Like, Primark is fine for some people but not for girls like us. Come with me to Oasis. My sister works there; I get a discount.'

'Please,' said Savannah. 'If Katie's shopping with anyone, it's going to be me.'

CHAPTER FOURTEEN

You know those great big groups of glamorous girls you see out on the high street sometimes? All long legs and long hair?

I was part of one!

And not on the outside, either, tagging along, trying to keep up. I was right there in the middle.

'So, Katie, help me out here. I'm playlisting my party and Paige and Sofie are worse than useless.'

We were trotting along the main road into town after school, Savannah managing to walk surprisingly fast given the height of her heels.

'Well,' I said, a tiny bit breathlessly, because really, going at that speed is unnecessary, even if the shops are shutting soon, 'I suppose it depends on what kind of vibe you're after.'

'It's going to be totally vibing,' said Sofie.

'Shut up, Sofie,' said Savannah. 'Katie is trying to speak. Also, vibing is not a thing.'

Amazingly, Sofie didn't seem to mind being told to

 135

shut up. And Paige didn't look especially bothered about being called worse than useless. I suppose you must develop a thick skin after an extended period of being around Savannah.

'If you want people dancing, then some proper disco would be good. Something like Chic, maybe Candi Staton. Then follow it up with—'

'Mm,' said Savannah. 'Complete yes. Make it up and send it to me, will you?'

I spent a moment trying to decide whether I fancied being Savannah's DJ and then decided that I did. Maybe she'd have those cool big headphones for me to wear.

Then . . .

'Lacey!'

Lacey was standing with her mum outside Tesco. When she saw us she turned away, but her mum gave me a wave.

'Katie! Sweetheart! You're a bit of a celebrity at the moment! Love the video. It's just a shame that Lacey couldn't have looked a bit more cheerful, isn't it?'

Lacey kind of growled.

'Are you out shopping? Lacey, you don't need to be

trogging round Tesco with me. Go. Go!'

Lacey did not look especially pleased to be joining us, but she stepped into place behind Paige.

'Enjoy yourselves, girls!' said Lacey's mum, disappearing off towards the trolleys.

'This is fun,' said Sofie. 'Where shall we go, Savannah?'

'Cindy's,' said Savannah.

Cindy's is the one good shop in Harltree, by which I mean, expensive. They stock Miss Sixty and DKNY and Michael Kors.

People like me don't go to Cindy's.

'We are so going to Cindy's,' I said.

'Fabbo,' said Savannah. 'I'm longlisting party dresses. I need to find something that really honours what it's like to be me, at my party.'

'But of course.'

'And you need to be thinking more about your look, Katie. Like, don't take this the wrong way, but right now you are so icky.'

'Thousands of people like my look!' I said, feeling the tiniest bit offended.

'Thousands of people have seen your look,' said Savannah. 'That does not mean they like it. And I am

 137

saying that as your biggest fan.'

There were two pieces of information there. I decided to concentrate on the second.

And yes, I was absolutely aware that Savannah was probably not my biggest fan, seeing as how she had only begun to notice me at the point where the video had happened. Still, though. You have to get your kicks when you can, and right now I was out shopping with a Harltree A-lister, going into Cindy's and being greeted by a woman who was very probably actual Cindy herself and being offered a free glass of fizzy water.

What wasn't to like?

'Darling Savannah,' said Cindy, whose face was as tanned as it is possible to be before becoming an orange. Then, 'Oh my goodness! You're her!'

'She is,' agreed Savannah.

'I am,' I said. 'Sorry, just to check, "her" being . . . ?'

'In today's paper,' said Cindy, spreading out the *Harltree Gazette* on her wooden counter. And there was a picture of me, right on the front page, with my crazy Jaz eyeliner and the headline:

HARLTREE GIRL HITS ONE MILLION

I showed the article to Lacey, who skimmed down and said, 'Why are you going on so much about our school music programme?'

And when I read it myself it did seem to be mainly about that. There was a nice bit about me and my influences, though, and actually, even the eyeliner looked OK, sort of rock and roll.

Savannah had gone off with Cindy to see some important new jeans, and Lacey said:

'Look, are you sure you want me here?'

'We're getting a taste of the high life,' I said.

Lacey looked a bit worried.

'It's just for now,' I said. 'Then we can go back to being the lowest of the low.'

'Speak for yourself,' said Lacey.

'Katie,' said Paige. 'What do you think?' She was holding up a black dress so small that for a second I thought it was a top.

'Blimey,' I said. 'Well, you could try it on, I suppose . . .'

'It's not for me!' said Paige. 'It's for you! I'm trying this.' She held up something gold and sparkly and about a sixteenth the size of the black mini-dress.

'That is gorgeous,' said Savannah.

'So nice,' said Sofie.

'It's very Paige,' said Lacey, which made me giggle, which made her giggle.

This was going to be fun.

And it was. Even when I got stuck in the mini-dress and Cindy had to come and cut me out again, which we all blamed on a dodgy zip and not the fact that Paige had clearly picked up something that was two sizes too small.

'You're so humble,' said Cindy. 'I'd have expected you to be this little diva, but you're not.'

'Mppppphhhhhhhh,' I said, still inside the dress.

'A million people,' said Cindy.

'Mmmmmmmphhhh.'

'And here you are in my little shop.'

'Mphhhh – oh, that's better, thank you,' I said, crawling out on to the floor and sucking in lungfuls of delicious, delicious air. 'I thought I was going to die in there.'

Lacey, meanwhile, wasn't taking any of this even slightly seriously, and had used the time while I'd been in my Lycra prison to pick out a selection of things that were simply absurd, like a green lurex playsuit and a leopard-print cape.

'Er, really?'

'Really,' said Lacey, looking longingly at a particularly bizarre ensemble. 'At least try it on.'

'I don't think so,' I said.

Normally, I would have done. Me and Lacey were very good at wearing silly outfits. But not here, not in Cindy's.

'But—' Lacey began.

'Katie,' said Savannah. 'Listen to someone with taste for one second, please. Like, I know you have this whole floppy baggy thing going on, but you are not actually *that* fat.'

'Er, thanks.'

'That's OK,' said Savannah. 'I mean, you could be way thinner if you just stopped with all the junk and found your inner model, she's completely in there, somewhere. But in the meantime, you should find your not-terrible bits and emphasize them.'

'My not-terrible bits.'

'Honour your waist, Katie.'

'Let's get this straight, Savannah. You are telling me to honour my waist?'

'Yes, babes.' She took a dress off the rack. 'With this.'

'This' being a floor-length navy blue dress with clever

straps that twizzled around the shoulders and in across the bodice in a way that I could already see would give me what Gran would call 'a proper bust'.

'That is so my party,' said Savannah. 'Go try it on.'

I checked the label. 'It's two hundred and twenty pounds,' I said.

'So?'

She looked at me, head cocked to one side, and I realized she wasn't quite seeing straight. I mean, she was seeing the me that had a million hits. The me that deserved nice things. The me that was going to her party.

What she *wasn't* seeing was the other me. The me that didn't have two hundred and twenty pounds. The me who lived in a falling-down house and had been known to eat pizza for breakfast.

'I can't afford it,' I said.

'Eew,' said Savannah. 'That is so upsetting.'

'Sorry, Savannah.' And I found myself feeling the tiniest bit of sadness. I don't know why. I mean, I'd never spent two hundred and twenty pounds on a dress before. I'd never considered that I might. I'd never even considered considering it.

People who spend lots of money on clothes are

idiots. Me and Lacey have always been extremely clear on that. It's way more fun to go to Oxfam on a Saturday morning and find something weirdly wonderful and take it home and lop the sleeves off and take the hem up and wear it loud and proud.

Except that, standing there, in the shop, with Savannah looking at me pityingly and the dress resting in my arms, all shimmery and clean-smelling, I was starting to think that maybe it wasn't more fun to go to Oxfam. That perhaps it *was* more fun to be Savannah.

At which point, I knew I had to get out of there.

'Oh, is that the time? I need to be back for dinner,' I said.

'Call me, yeah, babes?' said Savannah, who surely hadn't seen my phone recently because otherwise there is no way she'd have allowed anything so hideous to know her number.

'Will do.' Then, before anyone could say anything else, I bolted from the shop, with Lacey just behind me.

'What the—'

'Wait!' I told her, holding my hand up until we were around the corner. Then, 'Two hundred and twenty pounds!'

'Where does she think you'd get that kind of money?' asked Lacey. 'Honestly, she is so on Planet Savannah. She forgets the rest of us exist. Shall we go and get a Magnum?'

We went and got a Magnum. I let Lace have most of it. I was feeling kind of unsettled.

'Ooh look, Oxfam's still open.'

'Is it?' I said. 'Actually, I do sort of need to go home. I should send Savannah that tracklist before I forget it all.'

'Great,' said Lacey. 'Just me in there, then. Whatever I find, I keep!'

'OK.'

'Even if it's really amazing.'

'Fine.'

'Even if it would actually look better on you.'

'All right.'

'Katie! Can you honestly believe I'd do that to you?'

Which brought me back down to earth, and I smiled. 'You wouldn't dare. And I'll come in with you next week, once I've got my allowance. Got to get a party outfit, haven't I?'

'It's a date.'

Still, though. I couldn't help but think that once

you've been to Planet Savannah, even though it's weird and scary and incredibly expensive, you wouldn't mind going back.

So I was walking away from the high street back towards the main road through a particularly grotty bit of town. Once upon a time it must have been all right, as the road was cobbled in places, and a few of the buildings had beams and those nice windows you push up with both hands, that sometimes drop and try to snap your fingers off.

Anyway, because it was also Harltree, there were fried chicken boxes and cans lying around, and the shops were the sort I wouldn't even consider going into, a dodgy newsagent, something to do with second-hand computers and –

Oh no.

Amanda was just closing the door to Vox Vinyl. Adrian's place. Which was not where I'd intended ending up. Not now or ever. I turned around, but . . .

'Katie! Over here!'

'Hey, Mands.'

Her shoulders had been slumped, but now she was

bobbing about like a kite in a hurricane. 'You came!' she said. 'I'm sorry, you should've texted or something, another five minutes and I'd have gone.'

'I didn't know I was going to be here until now. Mands, the video! It's had a million hits! One million! And I'm in the paper!'

'Great,' said Amanda, clearly not listening at all. 'Are you coming in, then? There's loads to show you, I've got this noticeboard going, local bands can advertise gigs, look for new players, I've set up some cool lighting, and—'

'Maybe another time,' I told her.

'We're not in any rush.'

'Actually, now I've run into you, I wouldn't mind a lift back. I want to tell Mum about the hits. All one million of them. A million, Mands! A million people watching me! Us!'

Amanda slowly digested the news that I hadn't, in fact, come for a magical mystery tour of Adrian World and set off towards the car park. 'That's crazy,' she said.

'Are you saying I don't deserve it?'

She shot me a sharp look. 'Calm down, Miss Sensitive. I didn't say that, did I?'

I scurried along, trying to keep up.

'You're leaving early,' I said.

'I suppose so,' said Amanda.

'How come?'

'Adrian just told me I could go home, OK? God, Katie, why are you making such a thing about it?'

I hadn't been making a thing of it. But I would now.

'Did you mess up? Hey, you didn't nick something, did you?'

'What? No! Of course not!'

'Were you rude to a customer?'

She looked at her hands. 'Didn't exactly get the chance.'

This was not on. 'I can't believe he doesn't let you talk to customers! You know everything about everything, seriously, there's not a band in the world you can't go on about, and you're quite nice. He can't stick you in the stockroom like you don't exist. Do you want me to talk to him? I'm going to talk to him.' She unlocked the car and I slid into the passenger seat. 'You left a perfectly good job to go and work there, the least he can do is let you get on with it.'

'You are not going to talk to him, all right?'

'Oh, and you're just going to roll over and take it?'

 147

There was a short pause while Amanda swallowed an imaginary something. 'The reason I didn't get to speak to a customer isn't because Adrian wouldn't let me. It's because there aren't any customers.'

'Ah.'

'Yeah.'

'Well, he did sort of say not to jack in the cafe . . .' I stopped when I saw her eyes begin to glisten.

'You can't say anything. Not a word. Mum's got enough to worry about.'

'We'll talk about my million hits instead, shall we?'

'Good plan.'

Then she turned on the radio and we sang along to Adele all the way home.

In Honour

You said you were the one with taste
You said I should honour my waist
But I think taste is a thing you eat
And my waist says I need a treat

Gonna honour my hips
And honour my thighs
With ice cream, chips
And crisps and pies
Crisps and pies

You said being thin's a doddle
You said to channel my inner model
How did that model end up inner?
I guess I ate her for my dinner

Gonna honour my hips
And honour my thighs
With ice cream, chips
And crisps and pies
Crisps and pies

And come next week
I'll have a stew
With extra mash
In honour of you.

CHAPTER FIFTEEN

'Mum!' I was out the car and running up the road, my feet whacking the pavement, *swack thump swack*. I felt simultaneously as old as I've ever been and also about six. 'Mum! Muuuum!'

She was still in her uniform. 'Yes?'

'It's had a million hits! I'm in the paper! How cool is that?'

'It is very cool,' said Mum, which reminded me that Mum shouldn't really use words like 'cool'. 'We should celebrate. Let's celebrate!'

'Yes! How?' I thought of a Savannah-style festivity, with champagne and toasts and probably a firework display.

'Chinese?' said Mum.

'Takeaway?'

'No, ready meal. Adrian found a reduced box of them in Asda.'

I told her about the press conference and being invited to Savannah's party and how we'd been shopping and I'd seen a dress I liked, because you never know.

'That is a disgusting amount of money,' said Mum.

So, OK, sometimes you do know.

It was still pretty nice, though, especially with the smell of the black-bean sauce leaking out of the oven and Amanda humming 'Just Me' to herself as she got out the knives and forks.

'And let's have proper Coke,' said Mum.

We sat down at the table, the three of us, and smiled at each other.

'They played bits on the radio,' said Amanda. 'Annie Mac was telling people to go and find you online.'

'The consultant's daughter says to say hello,' said Mum. 'Apparently they're all big fans.'

Maybe fireworks are overrated.

Then:

'Evening, all.' He looked at the table. 'Enough for one more?'

There wasn't, but he sat down anyway and started digging into Mum's portion.

'Ade! We're celebrating. Katie's had a million hits!'

'Probably more, by now,' I said giddily. 'Probably quite a lot more.'

'Let's see then,' said Mum.

Amanda looked down at her phone. 'One million, two hundred and thirty-seven thousand, six hundred and twenty-six,' she said.

'I can't even slightly picture it,' I said.

'I think there's about a hundred thousand people living in Harltree,' said Mum. 'So imagine everyone in Harltree's seen it. I mean, everyone.'

I imagined the guy in the mobile phone shop, and all the other guys who worked in the mobile phone shop. And all the customers in the mobile phone shop. And everyone in all the other shops, up and down the high street. The women with the buggies and the babies in the buggies and every single person going in and out of the car park. All the streets, all the houses between there and here, the house with the funny turret thing and the flats they'd built in that old primary school and the posh houses with the great big gardens. And all the roads I'd never even gone down, probably never would go down, and the roads that came off those roads, and the roads that came off *those* roads, and each of them lined with houses and in each house, people, all those people, every single one of them watching me.

'Now times it by eleven,' said Mum. Then, after a few seconds, 'I know.'

'You have to remember this feeling,' said Amanda. 'For ever and ever.'

It was then that I noticed Adrian was shifting about in his seat. And I kept noticing him, picking at invisible bits on his jeans with those sausage fingers, rumpling what was left of his hair up and down and twiddling one of his supersized earlobes.

'So,' he said.

'What?' I replied, through quite a lot of beef chow mein.

'What are you going to do?'

'Remember this feeling,' I said. 'For ever and ever.'

'After that,' said Adrian.

'Er, I don't know.'

He was really rocking around now, so much so that I thought he might break the chair. 'This kind of thing, it just doesn't happen. You get record labels trying to break people for years, spending all this money, touring them, and nothing. And then in just a couple of days, you've got the kind of following some bands, even pretty big ones, can only dream of.'

I honestly didn't know what to say. '. . . So?'

'So I think this is an incredible career opportunity. And you have to take it.'

This was completely unexpected. Not just for me, but for Mum, too, who looked about ready to punch him.

'This isn't what we discussed.'

Wait, there'd been a discussion?

He looked at the table. 'No. It isn't. But—'

'But nothing. Katie is finishing her education and then she is going to get a proper job and, unlike *some people*, lead a decent and responsible life. She's got the brains to do so much more than this pointless—'

'My music is not pointless!'

'It's a hobby!' said Mum. 'And that is what it will remain!'

'Is this about Dad?' I said.

'It is about taking responsibility!'

'I'm a teenager! I don't have responsibilities!'

'You have the responsibility to finish school,' said Amanda in a way I don't think any of us found very helpful. 'And work hard and clean your bedroom and . . .'

Oh, honestly.

'I hear what you're saying, Zo,' said Adrian. 'But that

doesn't change the basic fact that what Katie has here is . . . something really incredible, and in my opinion she needs to embrace it.'

'*In your opinion*,' said Mum.

'Yeah. And I've been making some calls . . .'

Mum's face went purple, which sounds like an impossible exaggeration but isn't. 'Have you?'

'Yeah. And my old bandmate Tony, he's still in the business and he'd like to catch up, and meet Katie. Talk to her, find out what she's about—'

'Since when did I give you permission to start phoning people about my daughter?'

'That's not—'

'And how dare you send her off to one of those places on her own? She's a child, she can't be expected to make decisions like that . . .'

'Which is why I'll go with her!'

'Who said you could do that? I know how this goes. First, it's a recording here, a quick gig there. "Just a one-off, Zoe, and the money's great." Then suddenly they're running here, there and everywhere, and you don't see or hear from them in months. And then everything that was good, everything important, it gets . . . it gets . . . My family comes first, Ade. Before anything else.'

He held up his hands. 'I was only—'

'Before *anything*.'

'All right!'

She hadn't seemed especially interested when I'd basically come straight out and told her I couldn't stand the guy. Now that he was offering to do something nice for me, she was going mental.

I do not understand my mother at all.

Back upstairs in my room, I could still hear the shouting going on, little snippets drifting up the stairs like balloons, if the balloons were filled with misery. I heard, 'You do not go behind my back,' and, 'There is nothing more important than her education,' and 'This is Benjamin all over again,' which was not good news, considering what Mum thinks of Dad, and Dad almost certainly being the Benjamin in question.

I shut the door and turned it all over in my head. The facts were as follows:

1. 'Just Me' had had over a million views
2. Adrian could get me a meeting with a record label

3. Mum did not want me to meet with a record label

4. I had lied to Lacey about taking down the video.

Discounting number four, because really, I couldn't do anything about that right now, I was left with a sort of empty feeling inside. I could pretend all I liked that I didn't care about my song. Only, I did. I cared massively.

They'd played 'Just Me' on the radio. My words, out there in the world, doing their thing, getting into other people's lives. As though I'd diced up bits of my soul and chucked them over the airwaves like confetti.

And ... people liked it.

But Mum didn't care. Even Mands didn't seem especially bothered. How bizarre that the only person who seemed interested in my future was the one person I wanted out of it for good.

Still, if Mum said no, then that was that. I knew from experience that arguing with her wouldn't help. The only thing I could possibly do was go to meet this Tony guy without her permission.

But if I did that ...

Then I'd be, as McAllister would say, 'crossing a line'.

A line with signs all along it saying things like *Are You*

 157

Sure? and *Danger!* and *This Could Get Everyone into Some Pretty Serious Trouble.*

There was no way I'd do that.

'Adrian?'

'Katie!'

He was downstairs in the den, a bowl of crisps balanced on his stomach. I tried to think where I'd seen someone do that before, then I remembered; it was a photo of Mum, when she'd been pregnant with me.

I suppressed a full-body shudder and went in.

'I just came to say thank you,' I said. 'For helping me with my song. It's kind of incredible to think how many people like it.'

'Yeah, well. When I was in the band, we had a bit of a moment like this. We'd just recorded the single and we got booked to play on Des O'Connor, it was big. Primetime TV. We nearly . . . we might've . . .'

'Why didn't you?'

'The band split. That afternoon.'

'Creative differences.' I remembered.

'Yeah. Well, no. It was me. We were in the studio, doing the dress rehearsal and . . . I freaked out. Lost it. Told

Tony we should cancel the gig; that this wasn't for us. He didn't take it so well. Said I was mad. And maybe he was right.' He took a handful of crisps. 'And I said it would come round again, that I was talented, the opportunity would be back. And I waited. And . . . and here I am.'

'Here you are,' I said.

He seemed to sort of wake up. 'But you don't need to listen to me. You're young. You'll have plenty more chances.'

There was a very long silence.

'This Tony,' I said. 'Are you really still friends?'

'He sounded pleased to hear from me. Which was a bit of a surprise, given how we left things. Why?' He was looking at me, really looking. 'You still want to go and say hi?'

'Maybe,' I said. At which point I had this feeling like I was walking over the edge of a cliff, or something.

If Mum found out . . .

It would be bad.

Really bad.

This could even split them up.

No more Mum and Adrian.

Was I the sort of person who would do that?

 159

'Yes,' I said. 'I want to go and say hi.'

Apparently I was.

God.

He broke my gaze. 'I don't know.'

'Sorry,' I said. 'I know it's a lot to ask.'

'You know we'd have to . . . keep it to ourselves.' I nodded. 'It's a helluva risk to take. And for someone who doesn't even like me.'

So he'd noticed.

'I think you're great,' I said, trying to look into his eyes so he wouldn't know I was lying, and finding that I couldn't. Maybe if I just kept talking instead . . . 'I'm sorry if I've been grumpy. It's just the move, and school, and the divorce . . . I've found it very hard.' Which, come to think of it, was true. I had.

He nodded. 'Maybe we just need to get to know each other better. A trip to London could be just the ticket.'

Stay calm, Katie. Stay calm.

'Yes,' I said. 'It could be. We could hang out, maybe get some food, meet this Tony guy . . .' My voice was so high I sounded like a chipmunk. I tried to lower it, to regain a little sophistication. 'It would be pretty cool.'

'OK,' he said, hesitating. Then, as if he'd decided,

properly decided to go for it, 'OK! I'll tell him.'

He watched me doing a sort of dance of excitement, and his face . . . well. It made me stop. 'Are you sure about this?' I said.

'I suppose . . . I don't believe in regrets. I want you to feel like you gave this a shot. So if it doesn't work out, you don't spend the rest of your life wondering what might've happened.'

And for a second, or maybe even less, I understood what Mum saw in him.

CHAPTER SIXTEEN

I didn't sleep well. In fact I slept incredibly badly. Worse even than when I was little and trying to listen out for Father Christmas, or the nights after Dad had cooked his beef thing with all those peppers.

Because, the opportunity was there. This huge, glittering *thing* that I didn't even know I wanted, because I'd never thought I could have it.

To think that after all the hideous Mum and Dad stuff and Amanda and Adrian and the bus and school, that there was a way to turn my life into something new . . . into something good . . .

It was amazing, like a dream – ironic, given I hadn't slept at all.

'Morning, morning,' said Adrian. 'I'm frying eggs. Who wants a fried egg? Katie? Nothing like a fried egg, yeah?'

There was no way he could have been more suspicious, short of wearing a massive hat that said *I'm Hiding Something* across the front.

Incredibly, no one else seemed to have noticed.

'You all right to open up on your own today, Manda?'

'What? Oh my God!' She flushed a deep rose colour. 'Are you sure? That's such a responsibility.'

He grinned at her, and chucked a huge bunch of keys down on to the table. 'You'll be fine.'

'I'll do my best,' she said, all earnest and sincere. 'Thank you.'

I couldn't help rolling my eyes, just a little. Only, then I felt bad because Amanda bit her lip and looked down at her Curiously Cinnamons.

'Fried egg, Katie?'

'Yuk, no.' Just in time I remembered my new pro-Adrian status. 'Oh, all right, just one.'

He leaned in to plop an egg on to my plate, all wet and glistening and eggy, and as he did, he whispered, 'End of the road, 10 a.m.'

'What? 10 a.m. today?'

He was already back at the hob.

'What's today?' said Amanda.

'Oh, just . . . this . . . thing . . . I've got. With . . . Lacey.' When it comes to lying, I'm not the best.

'Adrian, can I play the new Michael Kiwanuka EP? Or would you rather I stuck to the official playlist?'

'Play what you like,' said Adrian. 'I mean it. You've got great taste.'

She practically danced on the table.

Meanwhile, I mooched off upstairs, wondering why Adrian wanted to meet me at the end of the road, like we were in a spy film or something. What with mooching and wondering and not being able to find any clean tracksuit bottoms, I didn't make it to the end of the road until nearly ten thirty.

Adrian was hanging out his car window. 'Quick! Get in! We're going to be late.'

'Late for what?' I asked.

'Top Music.'

'WHAT?' By now I was in the passenger seat, otherwise I might have collapsed.

'I fired off an email last night, got a reply straight back. He'd love to say hi. Of course, this is just a first meeting, so don't get too excited. These things take time. Lots more meetings. But it'll be interesting to hear what he has to say, yeah?'

'But, but . . . it's a Saturday. I thought people didn't work on Saturdays.' I was staring down at my scuzzy tracky bums and flaking nail polish. 'I haven't even cleaned my teeth!'

'We'll get you some Polos at the station.'

I had a quick look at myself in the car mirror, then wished I hadn't.

'So, Tony started Top Music a few years ago now. And I think it's doing pretty well, from what I can tell. Doesn't surprise me. He always had that kind of drive. Much more so than me.'

'And he's nice, right?'

'He's in the music industry,' said Adrian, doing a three-point turn in the middle of a really quite busy road. 'What do you expect? In fact, let's go over our non-negotiables. It's good to be clear on this kind of thing from the beginning.'

'Clear about what kind of thing?'

'Not missing school.'

'But—'

'You know what your mum thinks.'

'Dad wouldn't mind,' I mumbled. 'He'd let me miss school, if it was important. Which it is.'

'I'm not taking parenting lessons from a man who leaves his kids to go and live on the other side of the world,' said Adrian, which was the most he'd ever said about Dad. 'No missing school.'

I shoved myself down low into my seat. 'It's not going to be a very fun meeting, is it? If you go in and basically start telling him off.'

'Katie, I'm on your side.'

'But I can handle myself,' I told him. 'I'm really very sorted.'

We passed a sign for the station, and it occurred to me that I was on my way to London to meet a man at a record label.

'Katie, are you all right?'

'*Mnnnrg.*'

'You don't sound all right.'

'*Uwuuuug.*'

'Do you want me to pull over? Breathe, Katie. In out, in out. There we go.'

'Sorry,' I managed. 'It just occurred to me that I'm on my way to London to meet the head of a record label. *Whoooooah* – it's happening again.'

'In out, in out,' said Adrian. 'And, look, it's exciting. But it's not *that* exciting.'

'How do you mean?'

'He's not going offer you a deal on the spot, if that's

 166

what you were expecting. You weren't, were you?'

'. . . No.'

'Good. These things take forever, weeks of negotiation; they'll want to hear you play, maybe see what you're like in front of an audience. And that's if he wants you for the label, which he may not. Most likely it's just going to be a friendly chat so he can keep an eye on you, watch what you do next.'

'That's still cool,' I said, bravely.

'Don't be upset. That's more than most people get in a lifetime!'

Which was true.

Well, at least the hyperventilating had stopped.

London's brilliant. It's basically everything that Harltree isn't. It's so big that even familiar places aren't familiar really, at least not in a Harltree way where I know the exact location of every last puddle and the last major event was when they opened the new Tesco Metro.

There's just this . . . feeling about London. It's only a few miles from home but, really, it's another planet. London is dirty and dangerous and exciting and stuff happens there. Which is to say that even though I don't ever quite relax when I'm on the tube and I can't work out how anyone knows how to get the bus anywhere and when I get home and blow my nose my snot's grey from all the pollution, it's still my favourite place. It makes me want to write songs like 'Warwick Avenue' or 'Waterloo Sunset'. Only mine would be crazy happy-making and have a racing beat, with the kind of hook that makes you jump in the air and scream.

'Blimey, Tony's done well for himself.'

We were standing outside what must have been the biggest building on earth, and it was as though Adrian was literally shrinking. 'We were mates,' he said, like he was trying to convince himself it was true. 'He was a right one.'

I tried to imagine Adrian being mates with someone like I was mates with Lacey. Tried to picture him talking to them late at night on the phone, but I just couldn't. Possibly because mobiles hadn't been invented then. Maybe landlines hadn't either. He was pretty old.

'Are we going in?'

'. . . Yeah,' said Adrian, fumbling his way through the revolving door and tripping over his own feet.

I followed him in. The walls were made of this kind of

ripply, shiny stuff, and there were TVs inside the tables and on the pillars and, basically, all the places you'd least expect to find a TV. They probably had them in the toilets, too.

It looked like a film set. One all about a billionaire who lived in the future. On Mars.

We stood frozen for a second.

'Well?' I said.

'I haven't seen him since that afternoon,' said Adrian at last, and he looked down at the floor, which was glowing. 'We didn't part on the best of terms.'

'Chill,' I said. Not that I was feeling especially chilled.

He took a big breath and went up to the reception desk.

'Hi, love. I'm Adrian Lambeth and this is Katie Cox. We're here to see Tone.'

'Tone?' said the lady, who might have been a cyborg.

'Tone. Eee. Tony Topper.'

'Of course,' said Robowoman. 'Take a seat.'

We went and sat down and I watched the different TVs playing Karamel videos.

'They what you listen to at school?' Adrian said, nodding towards the screens.

'I'd rather saw off my own ears,' I said.

He tried to take his big jacket off and got an arm stuck, and, quite genuinely, it was the most embarrassing thing in the world. And then—

'ADE!'

The voice boomed across the reception, echoing up into the glass ceiling.

'T-Tony? You all right? It's b-been a while.'

'Mate! I didn't think you'd make it! How've you been?'

'This is Katie.'

'Hi Katie. God, it's been forever, Ade. How many years? Come through, come through. So, you married yet? Gemma's always asking about you, you old dog . . .'

London Yeah

Trafalgar Square and then Big Ben
Bond Street and Covent Garden
Greenwich and the Cutty Sark
And a really massively big Primark

Put your hands in the air
For London yeah

Camden Town and Kensington
Notting Hill and Wimbledon
Leicester Square and Regent's Park
And a really massively big Primark

Put your hands in the air
It's London yeah

Take me to the bridge
London Bridge
Or the Millennium Bridge
Either is good

Put your hands in the air
For London yeah

Put your hands in the air
It's London yeah

[Repeat until exhausted]

CHAPTER SEVENTEEN

Tony was about the same age as Adrian – whatever that was – and the same kind of build too: sort of fleshy, with a big face.

Which sounds like they were really similar, but they weren't at all. Because this guy, he was *rich*.

There are people at school who clearly have more money than me. You can tell because they come back from the Christmas holidays with a tan. And they have designer bags and clothes and will not stop talking about them. I know more about Savannah's Juicy Couture jeans than I do about some of my cousins.

Tony was different, though. He seemed rich all the way through. I'd hardly looked at him but I could see he had the sort of ripped, rumpled clothes you only get if you spend zillions of pounds on them; stubble far too exact to be an accident; and teeth so white it was bananas. Like he'd put some fake ones into his mouth and then coated them in Tippex.

'You look great,' said Adrian. 'Seriously, mate.'

'Ach, I'm just back from the Caribbean. You should've seen me before I went. Kurt, from Karamel – you know Karamel, right? – he was telling me I needed to take a break before I dropped down dead. And he was right.'

'You've been busy these last few years,' said Adrian, as we shot up two floors in a lift that was all mirrors, giving me a great view of the largeness of my behind. 'Since . . . since everything.'

'Yup, yup,' said Tony. 'Started the label small, meant to keep it that way, but Crystal Skye went platinum and then we just had to try and keep up, really. So –' Tony glanced back at Adrian as we swung into a corridor smelling strongly of perfume – 'you're not in the industry any more?'

'No, not any more,' said Adrian, and I wondered if Tony could hear the regret as easily as I could. 'Got the shop now, keeps me busy.'

'In town?'

'Just over in Harltree.'

'And are you married?'

'No ring yet, but I've got a great girl. Zoe, Katie's mum. It's not all this –' Adrian waved his hand around, as though some fingers could sum up the palace of amazingness that was Top Music – 'but I'm doing pretty well, given what happened.'

Tony nodded. Then, a second later, he was thumping Adrian on the back and saying, 'Good on you, mate. I'm glad it all worked out.'

We ended up in the biggest room ever. In the middle was an enormous table, with twelve huge chairs all the way around. On each wall was a big black-and-white photo: one of Karamel, one of Crystal Skye . . . And in the middle of the biggest table in the world was quite a small plate of biscuits.

'Take a seat, take a seat,' said Tony holding out his hand, which I think might have quite recently had a manicure.

I chose the chair closest to the biscuits and sat down.

'So, Katie. Here's my card; let me tell you a bit about us. We're Top Music. We've got some of the UK's biggest artists . . .'

'Wow,' I said, turning the card over in my hand. It said *Tony Topper, CEO, Top Music*. Then a phone number and an email address. In gold.

'We're doing great things, Katie, and we've seen your video. And we love it.'

So it turns out that dreams *do* come true. And not just the one where everyone in my form is laughing because Devi Lester has put squeezy mustard in my hair.

'You do?'

'We do.'

'Really?'

'Yes!'

Adrian cut in. 'What do you like about it?'

Tony looked me in the eye. 'You're so real, Katie. It *is* just you – your bedroom, your talent. We love it. Everything's so overproduced these days.'

'By you!' said Adrian.

Tony held up those well-groomed hands. 'Guilty as charged! But then, you haven't heard some of our guys in their raw state.' He leaned in and I caught a whiff of musky aftershave. 'Crystal Skye can't sing at all.'

I found myself giggling. 'She can't?'

'Nope. But you . . . you can sing.'

'Um, thanks.'

'So, tell me. Where do you see yourself going? Creatively, I mean.'

I took another biscuit. No one had ever asked me where I was going creatively. No one had ever cared.

'Er. Well, I've got lots more songs. I've been keeping them in a lyric book. Lots of lyric books, actually, because I've been writing songs for years and years.'

'Not planning on giving up any time soon, then?'

'No! In fact, I think I've got one in my bag somewhere . . . Hold on.' I had a look through my backpack. There was my English folder, a charger for my old phone, my sunglasses case, several biros, some broken headphones wrapped around my sunglasses and . . . there it was. With half a Mars bar stuck to the front.

I picked off the Mars bar and placed the book triumphantly on to the glass table.

'May I . . . ?' said Tony. He flipped through it. 'These look great.'

'So, OK, "Honour Your Waist" starts with a kind of strumming thing, just a few bars, then drums, one, two, one two three, and then the melody kicks in –'

'You're like a young Crystal Skye,' said Tony, closing the book and placing it back down on the table. 'So much energy. This is just the conversation I had with her, all those years back.'

'Thank you,' I said.

Tony glanced up at Adrian, and then smiled. 'Katie,

how would you like to join us at Top Music?'

'Hold up.' Adrian was leaning across, reaching for my book. 'Don't you want to hear any of this?'

'No need. I think I've heard more than enough. Katie?'

'That's . . . Sorry . . . I'm just a bit overwhelmed.' I took a biscuit, to calm my nerves. 'So, what does that mean? Like, if I go with you. Not that it's an "if". I mean "when". When I do, what happens?'

'You go into the studio and lay down "Just Me". We start thinking about a tour, shore up your fan base as soon as possible, an album . . . and then, if it all goes well, you, Katie Cox, are a superstar!'

A tour. An album.

'When can we start?' I said.

'We'll have to think about all this,' said Adrian. 'Won't we, Katie?' Then, to Tony, 'This is all going faster than we'd thought. Decisions like these can't be made in a rush. We'll go home, talk it through –' he threw me a panicked glance – 'really think about what's right. And Katie's not going on tour in term-time. That's non-negotiable.'

'What? We can totally negotiate!'

Tony spread his hands on the glass table. They were even more perfect than Savannah's, and she gets her nails done every Saturday morning in town. 'There's no hurry. You take all the time you need.'

'Thank you,' I said, casting a triumphant look in Adrian's direction.

'Although I would say that we shouldn't delay too long. I had a look at your analytics and your hits are still going up, but not at the same rate they were even a day ago. You can't afford to lose momentum on this. And of course we need to strike before the backlash.'

'Backlash?'

'It's inevitable. There'll be haters, trolls, maybe someone will send you a teddy bear cut in half or something, nothing to worry about. The important thing is to have a new story ready, regain control of the conversation . . .'

Adrian was tilting his head in a way that meant, 'Let's talk about this outside.' I pretended not to notice. And when that became impossible because it started to look like he was going to break his neck, I pretended I didn't get it. There was just no way I was going to leave the room. I mean, there are times you can go off into the corner to have a quiet chat about stuff, but while someone is offering you the chance of a lifetime is really not one of them.

'Do you mind if I just borrow Katie for a minute?' said Adrian.

'Sure, sure,' said Tony.

Adrian didn't ask if *I* minded, he just yanked me out the door, Tony politely pretending he hadn't noticed that I was being pulled along by the back of my jacket.

'I'm not sure about this,' said Adrian.

'I KNOW,' I said. 'Next time you want to talk to me, can you please not semi-kidnap me first?'

'I mean, with him. In there.'

I didn't have Adrian down as a complete idiot, just a partial one. Even so, I decided I would have to spell it out. 'He is offering to record "Just Me". He wants me to make an album. How is that not right?'

'It's too fast. It's wrong. We should be having a longer conversation. This is . . . It's not . . .'

'So you think that me being offered a record deal is wrong?'

'No. Yes! I think this deal is wrong. We should've approached a few other places, waited . . . Don't look at me like that. This is only because I care about you.'

'Thanks.'

'All I'm saying is that we leave it for now, go home, talk it over and go from there.'

'But you heard what Tony just said – there's no time for that! He wants to make me a superstar, but if we don't start now then it's over!' My voice cracked. 'Before it's even started.'

'You have the rest of your life to write music,' said Adrian.

'What, like you?'

Which even I knew was harsh.

I suppose that's why he didn't reply, but just looked down at his feet as I turned around and went back into the office, where Tony was waiting for me.

He smiled like everything was fine. Which it was, I told myself. Just because Adrian's having a freak-out, it doesn't mean anything.

'One thing,' said Adrian. 'Just, let me ask. What's the catch, yeah?'

'There isn't one,' said Tony.

'Course there's a catch,' said Adrian. 'I know you, Tony.'

It was one thing to say all this in private. It was another to say it to the man's actual face. And after he'd been so incredibly nice and basically offered me my dream on a plate. As well as a plate of really excellent biscuits.

Tony leaned back in his chair. 'You ever think about the old days, Adrian?'

'Nah,' said Adrian. 'I mean, yeah, a bit. A fair bit. Yeah.'

'Me too,' said Tony. 'We were something, weren't we?'

'Yeah,' said Adrian. 'We were.'

'I meant to say: I loved your work on Katie's video. Are you sure you've not been putting in a few sneaky performances over the years?'

'Ha!' said Adrian, looking away. 'I might've done the odd folk night down the pub. But—'

'Because your technique – it's old school. You're proper, Ade. You could show those Karamel boys a thing or two.'

'Well . . .' Adrian was grinning, even while trying not to. 'I suppose I could give them a lesson.'

'I was more thinking about a bit of session work on the album. Their new single has a retro vibe I think you'd really enjoy. We could make a thing of it. Feature you in the next video. Maybe not a bad idea to give the mums a reason to fork out for their little darlings, too. Fancy building a whole new fan base?'

'I'm in a very steady relationship,' said Adrian, but

I could see he was pretty flattered.

'Well,' said Tony. 'Just something to think about. Maybe while you're thinking about Katie.'

'Ach, I don't know,' said Adrian.

I must have sighed or made a bit of a noise, because something inside of him seemed to collapse, and he said, 'It's your call, Katie.'

Tony held out his hand. 'So, do we have a deal?'

I had this very, very strange feeling.

That if I said yes, I could stop being the girl who had a half-eaten Mars bar shoved into her bag. Who had lumpy skin and a messy room and a brick for a phone; who had to save up if she wanted to buy new strings for her guitar. The girl who'd never been further than Plymouth. I was about to burst free from her, leave her behind like an old skin.

Which should have been a happy thought. So I don't know why I shivered.

Actually, yes I do. It's because I was afraid. Afraid that this wasn't really *me*. The me that Savannah had sneered at, the me that got told off by McAllister, who missed her dad and was fighting with her best friend . . . the true me . . . she'd vanish. The me who wrote silly songs about the way she was actually feeling, she was going to disappear. And yes, she wasn't that cool, or exciting, but she was real.

And I didn't know if I was ready to leave her behind.

Then I thought, *Don't be so stupid. They're going to make you a star. This is your dream. It's everybody's dream.*

Who even was the real Katie, anyway? Just some girl with chipped nail polish and a songbook full of scribbles.

And so I shook his hand and said, 'Yes.'

CHAPTER EIGHTEEN

And then Adrian and me were back out in the street, both of us with hot red cheeks, half panting like we'd run a race.

'Is this really happening?' I said. 'I'm recording a single NEXT WEEKEND. In a studio. A proper recording studio. I cannot believe this is happening to me!'

Adrian smiled, and shook his head.

I couldn't seem to stop talking. 'I can't believe . . . we were just playing in my bedroom . . . messing around . . . and now . . .'

'I know!'

I was spinning, whirling about, bouncing off the cobbles like my feet were springs.

The sun's rays had gone golden and slanty, and Covent Garden was full of amazing-looking people, ramming the pavements outside every pub or hurtling towards the tube, and some guy with dreads was playing the saxophone and I just didn't want to go home. Not yet.

'I was thinking we could go for a bit of a walk

around?' I said. 'Since we're here.'

'Fair enough,' said Adrian.

Maybe he had a bit of that sunshine inside of him, too.

It would explain why he let me go into H&M, which had way better stuff than the one on the high street. This was just as well, as I had real trouble deciding between a turquoise belt and a bracelet. When I eventually came back from the till with the bracelet – which was the wrong decision, and something I still regret – I found him all worked up.

'There's a place just round the corner that sells guitars. Have we got time . . . ?'

Then we were in this guitar shop, and when he heard my news the guy behind the counter didn't mind that we clearly weren't going to buy anything, and let me play 'Just Me' on this electro-acoustic Fender in the most gorgeous deep orangey-red.

It somehow *sounded* orangey-red, too, or maybe that was just the feeling I had inside of me already, flowing through my fingertips into the strings.

After that, Adrian played a vintage Schecter, and then a Coronado Semi-Hollow. And then my stomach rumbled so loudly you could hear it even over the 1965 Gibson acoustic.

'Shall we get a sandwich?' he said. 'Or a pizza? Let's get a pizza!' He checked his wallet. 'Or maybe a sandwich.'

They have a Pret A Manger in Covent Garden, and we perched up on those high stools while the world flowed around us. I was like an island, surrounded by a churning sea of people. An island eating a salt-beef bagel followed by a chocolate brownie. Followed by another chocolate brownie, because we were celebrating, after all.

'You want this?' said Adrian, seeing me eyeing up his muffin.

'Are you offering?'

'No! But go on.'

'When you were in your band,' I said, 'what was it like?'

He chewed a crisp, thinking. 'A pain in the arse, mostly. We argued over everything. And the way it ended, I wouldn't wish that on anyone. But . . . I've never been closer to anyone than I was with Tony. I still miss that.'

'Not even with Mum?' I said.

There was a moment where he was clearly deciding whether or not to be honest. Then, he took another crisp. 'When I was in that band, it was us against the world. With Zoe, however close we get, you and your sister will always come first.'

He dropped me at the end of the road, then went off to the chip shop, leaving me to bounce up the lane on my own. It was the last part of the day, the blue of the sky fading down into a faint purple blush. I used to have some eyeshadow that exact shade. The one time I wore it, Lacey asked me whether I'd been punched.

The memory of it made me laugh, and then I was running, skip-hop-jumping, getting little bits of grit in my shoes and sending a fat bird twizzling up into the trees.

It's a secret, I said to myself. No one can know. Not yet. You've just been in town with Lacey. So calm down. Look normal. Be normal.

In fact, I remembered, Mum was on a long shift that day, so there wasn't any need to sneak around. It was only Amanda at home, and Amanda never noticed anything.

'Hey, Katie.' She was curled up on the sofa, watching TV.

'Hey, Mands. How was the shop?'

'All right.'

'Busy?'

'Not especially.'

Amanda hunkered down, as though she was trying

to disappear down between the cushions. Which was not a good idea. I'd seen what was in there when I'd helped carry it in for the move. Let's just say I put those cushions back in place and resolved never to lift them up again.

'So, has anyone else said anything about the video?'

She didn't even look away from the TV screen. 'Who?'

'I don't know. A customer?'

'No.'

'Oh. OK.'

I should have left her to it. Why didn't I leave her to it? Instead I said:

'So, Adrian took me to meet a record label today.'

'WHAT?'

At least now she was looking at me.

'And it was brilliant, Mands. It was this huge building in actual Covent Garden, and they had pictures of all their acts up, even yukky Karamel, and the guy, Tony, he was so nice and basically he offered me a record deal there on the spot and I said yes! And I'm going to record the single next weekend! How cool is that?'

'No WAY, that is AMAZING!' she said, and now she wasn't curled up any more, she was on her knees on top of the cushions, then tumbling on to the floor, then up on her feet. 'AMAZING AMAZING *AMAZING*!'

'Isn't it?'

'So Mum came round? Katie, we've got to get you into the shop for a gig, you could sign stuff—'

'Mum didn't come round. Mum doesn't know.'

Well, that threw a damper on things, I can tell you.

'Then why are you telling me this?'

'Because it's exciting.' *Because you are my sister.*

'You know what Mum said. We both heard her.'

'Yeah, but . . .'

'So why were you and Adrian sneaking off into London anyway? In fact –' she held up her hands – 'don't tell me. I don't want to know any more. I don't want to be a part of your . . . thing.'

Then, I got it. 'Oh. You're jealous.'

'No I'm not.'

'You are,' I said. 'You're jealous because it's my song and I'm going to be a proper musician.'

'I couldn't care less.'

'And because I spent the day with Adrian, not you.'

'You have no idea, do you?'

'Well, I'm sorry to have intruded on your love-in, but

 189

don't worry. You can have him back once the single's finished.'

The light seemed to dim, or maybe it was just because the ad break was over. 'You know they disagree. And you made him take your side and now what's going to happen? We have a home again.'

'A rubbish home.'

'A *permanent* home,' said Amanda. 'I thought you wanted that? And you're putting it on the line . . . for what?'

'I'm not putting anything on the line. Stop being so melodramatic.'

'But when Mum finds out—'

A thought gripped my neck with icy claws. 'You . . . you won't tell her, will you? If you tell her now it'll all be over before it's even started. You only get one chance, Mands, that's what I've realized, and if I don't take it . . .'

'This is a bad idea,' said Amanda. I waited. And waited. 'Fine. You win. I won't tell her, all right? But when this comes out – and it will – I am not getting involved.'

'I didn't need to tell you. I just thought you might be pleased.'

Her eyes were back on the television. And then I

thought of the other thing I'd come in to say. Which I probably should have got through first.

'Um, Mands. Can I borrow your phone? Sorry, I know it's not . . . only, I haven't checked my views on "Just Me" since yesterday, and as my new phone isn't—'

'Get stuffed.'

'OK!'

So I went upstairs and cleaned my teeth, which felt a bit pointless so late in the day, but they were feeling horribly furry. Then I lay down across my bed to try to get my mind around everything.

I had a record deal.

I was going to record a single.

And Mum was going to be fine with it.

The very second I got around to telling her.

That Belt

That belt
That belt
That turquoise belt
Six ninety-nine
And it could have been mine
With sparkly stones and bits of felt

Would've matched my leotard
Popped against my hot pink sweater
Here's the thing, that belt rocked hard
It would've made my whole life better

That belt
That belt
That turquoise belt
Six ninety-nine
And it could have been mine
With sparkly stones and bits of felt

Can only blame myself, it's true
As when I went to pay for it
I had to stand in a great long queue
Got distracted, bought a bracelet

That belt
That belt
That turquoise belt
Six ninety-nine
And it could have been mine
With sparkly stones and bits of felt

Would've made a whole new me
Could've been a fashion riot
But sadly it will never be
Because I simply didn't buy it.

CHAPTER NINETEEN

I love Lacey's house, I really do, although I have to say that I find being there a bit tense. Everything's so clean and nice and not-broken. She's got a special tap that has boiling water come out and an ice-cream maker and a white sofa without any stains on it whatsoever. Which I find quite stressful to sit on, but Lacey doesn't.

I aspire to being the kind of person who can sit down on a white sofa on a Sunday evening and drink Coke without having a breakdown.

'Just relax,' said Lacey, who is fully aware of my sofa issues, even if she doesn't support them.

I gripped my Coke can.

'It's really not going anywhere,' said Lacey, seeing the metal start to sink between my fingers.

Then Lacey's mum came in with – oh, *man* – two bowls of spaghetti bolognaise. 'We're watching *Jaws* later, if you girls would like to join us . . . ?'

'Katie can't watch *Jaws*,' said Lacey. 'It freaks her out. She'll cry and spill popcorn everywhere.'

'Can't have that, can we?' said Lacey's mum, glancing down at my bolognaise bowl.

Then she guided me over to a table with a perfect white tablecloth and white cotton-covered chairs.

'And I've got you chocolate ice cream with chocolate sauce for after.'

I wondered if it would be weird to ask her to put some newspaper down. Or if I could have mine in the garden.

Lace put me out of my misery. 'Can we eat upstairs?'

We took our bowls up to Lacey's bedroom, me sitting at her dressing table with my jacket spread out underneath, just in case.

Lacey ate sitting cross-legged on her white duvet cover and she didn't spill even a dot of sauce. I know this because she went off to the loo and I checked.

'OK, how weird was shopping with Savannah?' said Lacey. 'What is this world that she inhabits?'

'She needs to come with us to Oxfam.'

Lacey sat up, and if she'd been me she'd have spilt her dinner. 'You haven't invited her, have you?'

'No! Of course I haven't! Can you *imagine* . . . ?'

We imagined, and laughed.

'So here's what I don't get,' I said. 'How does a person be Savannah? Because I got a close-up look at her in the changing room and she is flawless.'

'What do you mean?'

'She's just perfect. All of her. I thought she'd have some monster birthmark or spotty armpits or something, but she hasn't.'

'Spotty armpits?'

'Yeah. From shaving them. Maybe I'm not doing it right.' I showed Lacey my armpits. 'See?'

'Yuk!'

'That is not how they look in magazines. Can I see yours?'

'No.'

'Please?'

'No!'

'I've shown you mine!'

'Did I ask to see your armpits?' said Lacey, who, to be fair, had not asked to see my armpits.

I sighed. 'Just think if Savannah had done the video. She'd probably have had three times as many hits as me.'

'How is that thing even still up?' said Lacey.

'Erm.'

I'd been thinking that I'd quite like to watch it again on her computer and see how the hits were doing but maybe it wasn't such a good idea.

'Perhaps *I* should be talking to Jaz,' said Lacey. 'Maybe I should offer her money or something.'

'Or, you could just get behind it,' I said.

'Huh?' She nearly dropped her fork. Nearly, but not quite.

'Look,' I said. 'Jaz isn't going to take it down. We know that. And a lot of people are watching it and they seem to like it and I know it's embarrassing for you but for me . . . it's kind of brilliant. Like, the best thing that has ever happened to me. And you're the best friend who has ever happened to me and I'd just really like it if you could be . . . OK.'

Lacey went to speak, and then stopped.

'And yesterday,' I went on, thinking it was now or never, or anyway, now or very, very soon and so it probably had to be now, 'I did something incredible. Me and Adrian, we went to see a record label.'

'WHAT?'

'It's called Top Music. They do Karamel and Crystal Skye.'

 197

'You hate Karamel. You say they are overproduced and have stupid hair.'

'Yes, but that's not the point.'

'That's not you, Katie. You're, like, all individual and bad make-up and split-ends-y.'

'I do not have split ends! Well, I do, but that's not the point. Which is . . .' I had to stop for a second to think what the point was. 'The point is, this is a really big thing for me. And I'd like it if you could be happy.'

'I am happy!' said Lacey.

She did not look happy.

'OK then,' I said.

We ate for a bit and then my bowl was empty, which was a shame, both because it meant I didn't have an excuse not to talk, and also because Lacey's mum is a good cook. One of those good cooks who goes in for small portions.

'The best thing,' I said quietly, 'is that he wants me to go into a studio and record "Just Me". As a single. I'm going to have a single, Lacey. Me.'

'Seriously?'

'Seriously.'

She swallowed and said, 'OK then. When are you recording?'

'Next Saturday.'

'Ah,' said Lacey. 'That might be a problem; I've got netball. Do you think you could make it Sunday instead?'

Which made no sense at all.

'Um, why does it matter that you've got netball?' I said.

'Well I can't exactly be in two places at once, can I?' said Lacey.

She went a very bright red as she said it, which meant that it was significant in some way. Only, I couldn't see how. I mean, it was *netball*. And Lacey played goal defence, which involved standing around for most of the match and then watching helplessly as someone taller than her got the ball through the hoop. Quite what this had to do with my recording career . . .

Oh.

'Can you make it Sunday? I can definitely make Sunday. Mum wanted us to go and see Auntie Lou but I'd much rather come up to London. Auntie Lou always makes me play with my cousin Andrew and he's at this funny stage where he just wants to list types of dinosaur.'

The wind blew rain against the window. Maybe it had been doing it for a while, but this was the first time I'd noticed.

'Lacey,' I said, trying to think of a sensitive way to phrase it, 'you're not . . . there's no reason for you to be there.'

'No reason for me to be there?'

'Well, no.'

Lacey looked around, as though she was trying to drum up a bit of support from her bedroom furniture. 'That is MY tambourine on the original.'

'What could I do?' I asked. 'Say I wouldn't do it without you?!'

'Yes!' said Lacey.

I'd been pretty patient. But *really*.

I couldn't put my one big chance of giving my life some kind of meaning on the line in order to include someone who didn't want to be in the original video anyway and had spent the last few days asking me to get it taken down.

There was just no way.

It was so obvious that it didn't even need explaining.

Except, apparently, to Lacey.

'Look,' I said. 'I'm sorry. But this is about being professional. And—'

'You don't think I'm professional?'

'Not at playing the tambourine, no.'

'Well, you're not a professional singer,' said Lacey.

'I'm about to be!'

'You wanted me to get behind you,' said Lacey. 'This is me getting behind you.'

'Which is . . . brilliant! And I'm so happy,' I said, trying to sound so happy. 'And I'll involve you, of course I will. I was planning to . . . thank you in the sleeve notes! Yes!'

'Great.'

'Great!' I was pleading now. 'So we're OK, are we?'

She sighed. 'I suppose so.'

'Does that mean we can watch *Mean Girls*?'

'I don't think I'm in a *Mean Girls* sort of a mood,' said Lacey. 'I'd like to go downstairs and watch *Jaws*. All right?'

'Um, OK,' I said, trying not to shiver. 'Let's do that.'

She got up off the bed. And then, at the same moment, we both saw, smack bang in the middle of her carpet, a big splodge of bolognaise sauce.

CHAPTER TWENTY

So the whole Lacey thing – and yes, I will admit that it had now become a proper actual thing – wasn't the best. Luckily, I had a million hits behind me, otherwise I might have been seriously upset about it all.

'Look,' I said to Jaz. 'It's gone up again. One million, three hundred and twenty-seven thousand, eight hundred and eighty-eight.'

'Yes, but have you seen my video of Nicole drop-kicking a brick?' said Jaz. 'She nearly broke her toe but it was so worth it.'

'Has it had a million hits?' I said.

'No, but we only put it up last night.' She unlocked her phone and turned away. Conversation over.

We got to school a tiny bit earlier than usual so the corridors were still pretty packed with the pre-assembly crowd, a bunch of year sevens here, a clump of year tens there, a slew of year thirteens blocking the way like a mountain range. I kept my eyes down, knowing they'd be watching, and blocked my ears with headphones. A load of people singing 'Just Me' was the last thing I needed.

'Katie Cox,' said the Head, who had chosen that particular moment to walk past.

'Yes!'

Knowing there would probably be more press stuff on the menu, I'd got into the bathroom before Mands could hog it and sorted out my face.

There'd been an exfoliating scrub, then a ten-minute mask. Then more exfoliating scrub, partly because there was still a bit left in the bottle, and partly because the mask seemed to have embedded itself into my pores and my cleanser hadn't been able to shift it. All this had made my skin a bit red, which meant I'd had to use plenty of Amanda's moisturizer, and this had given my cheeks a bit of a sheen, so I'd whacked on plenty of pressed powder to finish with. And I have to say, I didn't look actively worse than when I'd started, so, you know, result.

'Would you like me to talk to the papers again? Say a bit more about the music programme?' I said. 'Because I can. I don't think I quite covered everything the other day, but I reckon I could do it way better this time. I can work it in with my guitar playing and song writing and stuff, make it feel really organic, you know.'

'Katie,' said the Head. 'No earphones in school.'

'Oh.' I took them out. 'Sorry.'

And no one was singing 'Just Me', or at least, I'm sure they were, but not at that particular moment.

Phew!

So I managed to get through all that, just about, but there was still the form room to navigate. Which was definitely going to be tricky and embarrassing. Especially when I saw everyone was huddled around Savannah's phone and smiling and pointing.

'I know,' I said. 'Another hundred thousand hits. That's the entire population of Harltree all over again. On top of all the people who are already watching. Eeek.'

'Oh, hey, Katie,' said Paige.

Lacey did a sort of mini-wave.

'Dreamy, yes?' said Savannah.

'I've never seen anything more delicious,' said Sofie.

All right, maybe there was a *chance* that they weren't watching me.

'I want to lick the screen,' said Savannah.

More than a chance.

'Something more exciting than my song?' I said, jokingly. 'This had better be good!'

 204

'It is good,' said Sofie. 'It's Savannah's birthday cake.'

'Not the actual cake,' said Savannah. 'This one doesn't have a waterfall. But they're going to add that when they make it. Dad made them promise before he paid the deposit.'

I shuffled in between Lacey and Paige to see the screen. 'I was just wondering if you guys fancied another trip to Cindy's because I'm still considering that dress and, hang on, that thing is a cake?'

'Five tiers,' said Savannah.

'It has lights!'

'I know,' said Savannah.

'How can a cake have lights?'

'It plugs in.' She gave the screen a little kiss, as though it was a picture of her latest boyfriend.

Come to think of it, a cake boyfriend would be brilliant. You wouldn't have to worry about what it tasted of when you kissed, and if you ever split up you could eat it.

Was that too weird to be a song?

'I might write a song about that,' I said.

'So it's five flavours, obvs,' said Savannah. 'The bottom layer is red velvet.'

'Would you be OK with it being a song?' I said.

'Sure, babes. Then rose and pistachio.'

'I mean, a lot of people might hear it.'

'And then cherry vanilla swirl.'

'Because,' I said loudly, 'of how I'm going to record a single! I have a record deal and I am going to record a single. Me!'

Well, that shut her up, and with two tiers still to go.

'For real?' said Sofie, and finally it seemed like I'd pulled her attention away from Savannah's catering arrangements.

'Totes,' I said, which is the first time I've ever used that word and also, I suspect, the last. 'I went into Covent Garden and I met with the head of Top Music, they do Crystal Skye and Karamel and stuff.'

Savannah perked up.

'Can you get us free Karamel tickets? A backstage pass would be the most perfect birthday present.'

'I bet I can,' I said.

Savannah smiled the first genuine smile I'd ever seen from her. I know it was genuine because her forehead scrunched up and she looked a bit gummy. Savannah *never* looks gummy.

'Babes, if you can do that, then I will . . . I will . . .' She searched around for the most grateful, the most amazing, the most generous thing she could think of. 'I will invite you to my party.'

'I thought I was already invited to your party?'

'Oh.' Savannah was clearly considering uninviting me so that she could reinvite me on the condition that I got her some Karamel tickets.

'I'll definitely get them for you,' I said. 'I don't know if it'll be in time for your birthday, though.'

'Well,' said Savannah, looking the tiniest bit deflated, 'late is better than never. Let me know when you have dates, yes?'

'I will,' I said.

'Thanks, babes.'

'So I probably shouldn't talk any more about how the meeting went or anything,' I said. 'But I suppose, just to finish off—'

'You've genuinely got a record deal?' said Sofie.

'Yes. With the people who do Crystal Skye and Karamel. Yes I have.'

'Even though she hates Crystal Skye and Karamel,' said Lacey.

'She hates Karamel?' said Savannah. Then, to me, 'You hate Karamel??'

'I hate boy bands,' I said. 'And Karamel are a massive great big boy band, so yes. I hate them.'

'I still don't get why you'd record a single with a record label when you can't stand any of their music!' said Lacey.

I thought of that huge glass building and the posters and the incredibly expensive biscuits. I thought of Tony's eager expression. I thought of that receptionist with perfect make-up, and Covent Garden, and how, even with a million hits, my friends clearly still considered me slightly less exciting than a cake.

'You wouldn't understand,' I said. 'It's an industry thing.'

'If you say so,' said Lacey.

'Anyway. The point being, we're recording the single this weekend!' Lacey looked away. 'And after that, who knows? I suppose we'll make a video and then perhaps there'll be an album. My album!'

The door bounced open and there was McAllister, looking mightily annoyed, which is just her normal expression, but still. 'Pray what are we all discussing so intensely when we should be on our way to assembly?'

'Katie's got a record deal,' said Sofie.

'That is very exciting,' said McAllister, her eyebrows moving fractionally higher in a way that I'd never seen before, which I suppose meant she was genuinely excited. 'Now, assembly. Lacey, cheer up for goodness sake. And Savannah, those earrings are coming off right now or I will take them home and give them to my niece.'

Cake Boyfriend

Pat-a-cake
Pat-a-cake
Baker's man
Bake me a boy as fast as you can

Give him fudge for hair
And frosted blue eyes
And finish him off with
Vanilla sponge thighs

My cakey boyfriend
Oooh my cakey boyfriend
My bakey cakey boyfriend
Oooh my cakey boyfriend

And when we kiss
It'll be so fun
I'll nibble his earlobes
And bite his tongue

My cakey boyfriend
Oooh my cakey boyfriend

My bakey cakey boyfriend
Oooh my cakey boyfriend

He'll have a sweet boy heart
But if we ever disagree
Gonna cut him into slices
And have him for my tea

My cakey boyfriend
Oooh my cakey boyfriend
My bakey cakey boyfriend
Oooh my cakey boyfriend

And when he's gone
It won't much matter
You can bake me another
From the leftover batter

My cakey boyfriend
My cakey cakey boyfriend
Oooh my cakey boyfriend
My bakey cakey boyfriend.

[Repeat to fade]

CHAPTER TWENTY-ONE

It seemed like Saturday would never come round, but then luckily it did, or I might just have exploded through an excess of nervous energy. Even things that normally made time go quite fast, like watching TV and sleeping, felt plodding and gloopy, as though the world knew I wanted to hurry up and had decided to go into slow motion.

As I say, though, Saturday did eventually put in an appearance. It began, as all Saturdays did, around the kitchen table, with Mum picking up mouse droppings from the floor and saying, 'I'm going straight from the hospital to karaoke, if that's all right?'

We all said it was.

'Anyone doing anything fun today?'

'Well,' said Amanda. 'I am going to run the shop. Adrian's shop. I will be running it.'

'Good for you, my love,' said Mum. 'So you're not working today, Ade?'

'Thought I'd take Katie out for the day,' said Adrian.

'Get to know each other a bit. Yeah. Mmm.' He was such a bad liar. I had to take over.

'We decided we'd do a bit of bonding,' I said. 'Go for a drive, maybe get some lunch or something.'

Mum looked from me to him and then back again. Of course she didn't believe us. We were so blatantly lying. I braced myself . . .

'Finally!' said Mum. 'Two of my favourite people in the world have started getting on.'

'Er,' I said. 'Kind of.'

'What are you going to do?' Mum said. 'Tell me. I want to be able to picture you together.'

'Just go into town,' I said.

'Town!' said Mum.

'. . . Eat a pizza?'

'Pizza!' She went to her wallet and fished out a twenty. 'Spend it all.'

'It's really not that big a deal,' I said.

'It is,' said Mum. 'If I could've had one wish in the world it would have been for the two of you to be friends. Now, I'm going to have a shower. If anyone touches the hot-water tap I will personally come and drown them.'

She went, humming the chorus of 'Natural Woman'

  213

and, after a moment, Adrian followed.

Manda's nails came digging into my arm.

'You have to stop this.'

'The shower?'

'The lies to Mum.'

'I told Tony yes,' I said.

'So tell him you've changed your mind. Or tell her. Tell her right now and see what she says.'

'You know what she'll say. She'll say no. And –' I was surprised to find I was on the verge of weeping into my Pop-Tart – 'I want to see what happens. It's exciting. It's the most exciting thing that'll ever happen to me and if I pull out now, that's it. Over. Finished. Just the whole rest of my life with nothing to look forward to. Just like everyone else.'

'That is an extremely unhealthy way of looking at it,' said Amanda. 'Honestly, Katie, you can't pretend your life is already over. You've not even left school.'

'FINE.' And now I wasn't sad any more, just angry. 'I want to do this because it will be COOL. All right? I want to sound amazing and look amazing and for people to buy my album and listen to my songs and think, "These are brilliant." Because I am a selfish, horrible person. And maybe you think I ought to be content with getting the bus to school every day and having my bra strap pinged and egg mashed into my hair and listening to Savannah's party plans. But honestly, I think I might be happier at least having a go at something else.'

Mands put down her mug and left. But I knew she wouldn't tell Mum. So I suppose I ought to have felt good about our little chat.

Somehow, I didn't.

I'm a star, I said to myself. *I am an artist. I am going to record my single. Like Adele and Rihanna and Jessie J. I'm doing this. It is real. This is me, on my way to London. To sing.*

I kept this up in my head all the way there, and I was so hyped by the time I got to Tottenham Court Road, I could feel my fingers trailing fairy dust all over the ticket barriers.

Adrian, on the other hand, seemed edgy, and every time he opened his mouth, a downer dropped out.

'There'll be a lot of people from the label there,' he said. 'I know you liked Tony and he seemed laid-back, but take it from me, the studio's very different from the office.'

'Huh,' I said, not really knowing what he meant, and not much wanting to think about it.

'See, they'll have their own ideas,' said Adrian. 'And sometimes that's great! A collaboration!'

'OK,' I said, navigating my way past a woman with a suitcase who was completely blocking the way out.

'Sometimes, though, it's not so good. You don't want them to over-commercialize your sound. I mean, a little smoothing out, that's all well and good. But . . .'

'But what?'

'You're *you*, Katie. And that's not very Top Music.'

'What are you trying to say?'

'You're special. Don't let them make you into something you're not.'

'Which is . . . ?'

'Slick. Auto-tuned. You know.'

'Maybe I'm OK with that,' I said. 'Seriously, what is it with people thinking I don't deserve the full treatment?'

He stopped. 'Is that what you think? That you don't deserve it? The point is that you don't *need* it. Katie, maybe you don't know it, but there's no one out there right now even half as good as you. You know why people keep clicking on the video? Because you're Katie Cox! So enough with trying to be someone else, all right?'

'Oh,' I said, swinging my guitar straight into a surprisingly grumpy busker.

After a few minutes apologizing, which didn't work, and a fiver from Adrian, which did, we got far enough away for me to say:

'Look, I get that you're worried. But let's just see how it goes, shall we?'

'Yeah.'

'But –' and I had to glance down at the pavement because it was difficult to say – 'I appreciate that you care.'

'Nice one, Katie,' said Adrian, looking like he might be about to go for some kind of hug, and then, thank the Lord, we reached a small doorway with a line of buzzers, one of which said *SQ Studios* and the conversation was over.

Despite what Adrian had said, it was just Tony who was there to meet us, rising up out of a chair shaped like an egg to grab my hand and tell me how excited he was.

The whole place was smaller than I'd thought it would be. Down at the end of a long flight of steps, there was

217

this strange sealed-in world without windows, sort of shabby and worn, with things stacked up against other things and peeling-back carpets. And while I could mainly smell Tony's aftershave, there was just the faintest tang of mould, like dark clouds lurking on the horizon at the end of a sunny afternoon.

Just nerves, I told myself, noticing how dry my mouth had gone, and giving my throat a very subtle clear. And then another one, and another, until Adrian handed me a bottle of water.

'Takes me back,' he was saying, nostrils flaring as though he was sort of inhaling the scene. 'Hey, Tone, maybe it's my mind playing tricks, but, isn't this where we recorded back in the day?'

'It is,' said Tony. 'The very same studio. I thought it would be . . . poetic.'

Which explained why everything was so dark and poky when I'd been expecting more of a Top Music reflective-surfaces vibe.

'What sort of stuff were you planning?' I asked. 'Because I don't want fifteen backing singers or a string quartet or anything.' I could see Adrian nodding.

'Right now, it's just you and your guitar,' said Tony,

motioning me down yet another set of stairs. 'We can always put more on later.'

'Or not,' I said. 'If it doesn't need it.'

'It's entirely your call.'

'That doesn't sound like you, Tony,' said Adrian, but I guess his words got lost in a load of doors opening and closing, because he didn't get a reply.

Then, we were in a room with a glass wall, where a man sat at a desk covered in knobs and dials and lights and sliding things.

'How does it feel, Katie?' Tony's smile split his face in two. 'How does it feel to be recording your first single?'

'It feels . . .' I tried to put into words the electricity sparkling down into my fingertips, the way my stomach felt as though I was just getting to the top of a rollercoaster, the grin that kept tugging at the corners of my mouth.

'Don't tell me. Tell Adrian. He's the one responsible for all this.'

I turned, wordlessly, to Adrian, and Tony said, 'Look at her, Ade. Remember that feeling?'

'I do.'

'I have to get a picture,' I said, getting my new phone

out. 'The girls at school will lose it when they see me in here.'

I turned it over, looking for the camera. Oh. Yes. The stupid thing didn't have one.

'Adrian . . . your phone . . . can I just take a quick selfie?'

'What's a selfie?' said Adrian, and I decided to leave it.

'Katie,' said the desk guy, while simultaneously pressing some of the buttons on his desk, 'I'm Moe. Want to go tune up? It's through there.'

I unzipped my guitar. Having it in my arms felt easier. *I can do this,* I told myself. Moe followed me in and started fiddling around, putting headphones over my ears and making the microphone stand higher and lower and then higher again.

'Happy?' He looked at me like he felt sorry for me. Like how Savannah looked at me, only his eyes were kind.

'What artists have you had?' I asked.

'Recording here? A few biggies. Kylie did some bits; Elbow, they were a laugh; Lorde, we loved her . . .' He touched my shoulder. 'Relax. You're going to be fine.'

He was gone, shutting the door behind him. The room was now very, very quiet. Not the deep silence of the countryside at night or the scratchy hush of exams. This silence was flat and complete. As if someone had turned off my ears.

'Katie? Can you hear me?'

The words came through the headphones, but honestly, it was as though they had been injected straight into my brain.

'Yup.'

My voice had never been so clear. I could hear every last part of it, all the little creaks and clicks, the slight wet noise my tongue made against the roof of my mouth. I'd always thought of it as smooth, something that flowed, but now, close up, it was like wood: grainy and knotted and full of splinters.

'Katie, hi?' Tony, this time. 'Ready to have a go?'

I strummed a chord, and then another.

'Let's do a quick run, see how we get on, shall we?'

Then my fingers were scattering notes this way and that, as the tune rose up in my throat.

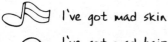 I've got mad skin

 I've got mad hair . . .

When Adele had started out, she'd have been just the same as I was now. Standing in a studio, full of music.

And, call me crazy, but it was as though they were all there, my idols, lining up just behind me, cheering me on. Kate Bush, her arms wrapped around Amy Winehouse's eeny-weeny waist; Dolly Parton, all boobs and hair; Joni Mitchell and Taylor Swift; Björk, who was for some reason dressed as a swan . . .

Adrian winked at me through the glass, and as he did, I felt my heart leap.

I've got mad love
I've got mad hate
I've got all my life to come and I just can't wait
And here's the thing, I think you'll agree
We're all in this together. It's not just me.

CHAPTER TWENTY-TWO

Later, much, much later, I was back in my bedroom. My bones were still vibrating with the memory of it all, so much so that I couldn't quite seem to sit still and kept pinging between my bed and my desk and the window and the floor, round and round and round.

There was the same tangle of clothes at the end of my bed, the same weird stain on the ceiling, the same old plate of pizza, with its ever-increasing mane of green fur. Nothing had changed, but somehow everything had. Which I suppose is what it will feel like when I actually have my first kiss, an event so far distant that they will most likely get a man on Mars before I manage to get one anywhere near my mouth.

I so wanted to tell Lacey about the day. How Moe had clapped me on the back and said that I'd played a blinder. How they'd asked me if I was hungry and brought me a chicken wrap when I'd said I was. How they had a big jar of pencils on the desk all with *SQ Studios* written on the side and how I'd pinched a couple at the end, one for me and one for her.

But that was old Lacey. It would take more than a pencil to get her to like me again.

Still, she'd come round. And the pencil would keep.

How long until a pencil goes off?

There was at least one person I *could* tell. One person who was scheduled to talk to me, who would be obliged to ask me how my day had been and listen to the answer.

I looked at the clock again, and again and again and again, until finally, *finally*, it was time to talk to Dad.

'Katie!'

And oh, but it was good to hear his voice. Like buttered toast on a cold Sunday afternoon. Like a hug. Like . . . Dad.

'So, my little pop star, I've been hearing great things! *Let's all sit down and have a cup of tea!*'

'You've seen the video, then.'

'Have I seen it? It's all I see! I put my email on, I get links to you. And people asking about you. Did I know my Katie was all over the internet, what do I think, can I get her to sign stuff for the girls at the store?'

'It's called a shop, Dad.' Since he'd crossed the Atlantic, he'd developed a nasty habit of referring to sidewalks

 224

and zucchini. 'People are listening to me in California? I can't believe it.'

'You'd better believe it.' He inhaled. 'And that's Adrian, huh?'

'Yup.'

'Bit of a sloppy pianist, if you ask me.'

'He's all right.'

But Dad was still going. 'Nah, he's rotten. And his dress sense isn't much better. I'd have thought your mother might have gone for someone a bit more . . . well, a bit less . . .'

The way Dad bangs on about Catriona, I couldn't resist taking the opportunity to get my own back, just a tiny bit. 'He might be doing some session work on the new Karamel album.'

'No way!' Dad sounded genuinely upset.

'It's true.'

'I can't remember the last time I worked with anyone under the age of twenty-five.'

'Come back here then,' I said. 'I'll talk to Tony, see if he can't get you in on it as well. I'm sure you could stay on the sofa.'

'Ah, you know, I said I'd help Catriona set up her new

studio. Honestly, though, that Adrian bloke, he's a piece of work.'

'But you thought *I* was all right?' I asked. Which was fishing, I know. But . . .

'Katie, you were wonderful.'

At last, a family member who appreciated me. It put me in such a good mood that I even asked, 'So how is Catriona?'

'She's great! She's just started two more classes, so she's incredibly busy, but good busy. And she's been making me these terrific hot chocolates, sweetened with this Stevia stuff, it's like sugar, only it's not sugar . . .'

This went on for a while. And reminded me why I don't normally ask.

'So, you should know,' I said, 'I'm going to release the song as a single.'

'One of the girls was saying that's exactly what you should do. Everyone's at it these days; apparently it's really easy. Just a few clicks, and maybe I won't have to send you all that maintenance money. Joke!'

'Ha ha. No, it's with Top Music, they're a proper record label. We went to London today to record it.' I had this sudden flash of fear that maybe he wouldn't be OK with it. That he'd freak out, break his code of silence with Mum and –

'That is fantastic news! FANTASTIC!'

'Y-you think so?'

'Of course! Top Music? They're huge!'

'You're not worried? You don't think that it's basically a bad idea?'

'Of course not. Stop being so negative!'

'Just, Mum's been a bit, er, funny about it. Mum and Lacey, actually. And Adrian's been going on and on about how they were going to make me miss school and change my sound and how stressed out I'd be and that the whole thing would be a fight. But it wasn't like that at all! Tony, he's the head of the label, he's been completely nice and he let me record it exactly how I wanted. I did it in three takes. Literally!'

'Of course you did.'

'So you're not going to jump on a plane and ground me or anything?' I said.

'Katie,' said Dad. 'You're happy, right?'

'Very.'

'Why would I mess with that? You go out there, do what you want to do, then make sure you get on the

227

phone and tell your old dad all about it.'

'OK!'

Clearly, this was the correct reaction. The normal reaction. The reaction of someone who cared about me.

We talked for a while after that, about a scorpion Dad had found under his car and the ins and outs of opening a Pilates studio in a neighbourhood that already had three Pilates studios.

And I told him how great our new house was and how much I was enjoying the bus ride to school and how everyone was getting along so well. By the time I put the phone down, I was exhausted with the effort of smiling so hard. A smile, due to recent broadband restrictions, that Dad couldn't even see.

'I'm glad you guys are happy,' he said. 'When I was around, everything seemed so hard. But you're making it look easy!'

For a second I faltered. And for some reason, Adrian's words came back to me: *I'm not taking parenting lessons from a man who leaves his kids to go and live on the other side of the world.*

'I wish you could come and see us,' I said. Then, quickly,

before I could change my mind, 'It's just, I miss you so much.'

'You don't need me,' said Dad. 'I'd just get in the way of this new career of yours.'

'Um, OK.'

'Bye, Katie. Speak soon.'

'Speak soon, Dad.'

There was something wrong with Amanda. I could tell because she wasn't eating her toast and because she'd not bothered getting dressed. Oh, and because she was crying.

'What?' I said, quite quietly, then, when she didn't reply, '*What?*'

'There's just no point,' she said.

'What do you mean?'

She looked around. 'Just . . . this. I don't know.'

We both went quiet as Mum bumbled over to the back door, doing something with a load of plant pots. Once she was safely outside, Mands wiped her nose on the back of her hand. 'Don't you ever feel like things are just a bit hopeless?'

'This isn't like you,' I said. She shrugged. 'Come on,

there's loads to be happy about! The sun's shining. And we live in a world of opportunity. Anything can happen! Seriously.'

'Anything can happen?' said Amanda, slowly. 'Anything?'

'Miracles are possible. I am literally proof of that. Two weeks ago I was nobody. And now . . . !'

'You are the exact same person that you were two weeks ago,' said Amanda. 'Just, more people have seen into your bedroom. Which, by the way, is a health hazard.'

Arguing with her was clearly not going to get me anywhere, so instead, I said, 'Has something upset you, Mands?'

'Yes. Yes, actually, it has.'

I waited, but all I got was more sniffing. 'Is it me?' I said, dropping my voice so that there was no way Mum could hear, even though she was safely at the end of the garden. 'Because I'm going to tell her. I just want to wait a tiny bit longer, just so she can hear how amazing the single is and be proud of me and then maybe she'll understand, that's all . . .'

It wasn't helping. Watching Mands weep and weep made me feel so terrible that I was on the verge of getting up and fetching Mum and telling her everything. Only then she said:

'It's the shop.'

'What, Adrian's Disaster Emporium of Hopelessness?' I laughed with relief. 'I mean, seriously, what is with that place? Who even goes into a shop and buys music any more?! It's like he's literally trying to go bust.'

'SHUT UP, KATIE.'

Which was unexpected.

All the softness had gone from her expression. In fact, in maybe a millionth of a moment, she'd gone from teary big sister to red-faced spitty-mouthed monster.

'The shop *is* going bust. And Adrian won't tell Mum because she's so into the idea that he's the head of this retail empire.'

'But . . . can't you . . . just . . .'

'You think you know everything, just because you've been going up to London. You know nothing. Nothing. OK?'

I just stared. Maybe my mouth flapped open and shut a few times.

'Because I have TRIED. That shop was *my* dream, K. You know about dreams, right? I thought, maybe, if it was

 231

run by someone who was really passionate about music, who could talk to customers about bands, play them stuff they'd love, then maybe it could work. That I'd have unsigned groups do new-act nights and a noticeboard where people could sell second-hand guitars and bands could find new drummers and we'd have regulars who'd buy up all the rare vinyl and maybe we'd arrange coach trips to festivals and do a podcast of things we were enjoying and yes, Katie, I *know* no one buys music in a shop any more but I thought maybe I could change that. And now Adrian's business is going to go bust and that's my dream over. Done. Finished.'

'But everything you just said, they're all great ideas. It deserves to work. I mean, you do. It sounds like you're being brilliant. Incredible. He's lucky to have you.'

'Maybe,' she said, and now the tears were back. 'But it's not enough. I'm glad you're getting to live your dream, Katie. But it doesn't mean I will.'

CHAPTER TWENTY-THREE

There's a patch of grass around the back of the school labs that's supposed to be a wilderness garden.

I've never quite known what a wilderness garden ought to look like, but I'm fairly sure no one meant for it to turn out how it did, which was this dark, damp corner of the school with moss instead of grass and a big row of recycling bins. Once, Lacey swore she saw a bluebell growing there, but it was so obviously wishful thinking on her part that I didn't even consider believing her.

Being totally honest, things between me and her were not good. Just how not good, I wasn't sure, as she wasn't especially talking to me. I don't think she was actively *not* talking to me, as she answered my questions and replied to my texts. But ever since *Jaws*-gate I was aware that if someone came and tested our friendship levels, they'd have found we were running pretty low.

So I'd brought her outside in order to try a bit of BFF-style bonding. To really talk about our feelings, get close, and open up to each other in that way only besties can.

'Um,' I said.

'Mm,' said Lacey.

'Er.'

'Oh look,' said Lacey. 'There's Savannah. Shall we go and sit with her?'

'But, but . . .' I began. Then, because Lacey was already parking her behind on the grass, 'OK, then.'

The Savannah-Paige-Sofie beast had found the one patch of sunshine in the whole area and had stretched out its six very long, very brown legs.

Come on, Katie. Spread the love.

'Hey, everyone. Mind if me and the very awesome Lacey Daniels sit with you? She's so great.'

Which earned me some very strange looks.

'We're party planning,' said Sofie.

How much planning could one party take?!

'How much planning can one party take?' I said.

'Just because *your* parties are three people dancing to an ancient *NOW* album doesn't mean everyone else's are,' said Lacey, in a way that, frankly, sounded a little critical.

'Mellow down, girlfriend,' said Savannah. Then, to me, 'Have you got my Karamel tickets? How was the recording? And have you got my Karamel tickets?'

'Sorry, no tickets yet,' I told Savannah. 'But the recording was amazing. It was in this little studio in Soho and I did it in three takes.'

'I bet you have the most amazing pictures,' said Sofie.

'It's annoying, but actually, I don't. Stupid Neanderthal phone. But it was so interesting down there. They had all these framed platinum albums on the walls and a signed photo of the Rolling Stones. I mean, I'd have paid just to look round, and there I was, actually getting to record my own music.' I shook my head. 'It blows my mind.'

'Amaze,' said Savannah, wiggling her perfect little toes. I noticed that each nail had been topped with a sparkly stone. 'You know what? Even though you don't have any Karamel tickets for me, I think we should play your single at my party.'

'That would be pretty groovy,' I said, which was supposed to sound casual and laid-back and super-chilled but didn't due to my using the word 'groovy'. I mean, who says that? Other than me? 'I'll send you the MP3.'

'Can we hear it now?' said Paige.

'I haven't got it yet,' I said. 'Sorry.'

'But I thought it was all recorded?'

 235

'These things take time,' I told her.

'So you don't know when it's out?'

'Er, no. They didn't say. Soon, though. Because of momentum.'

'But it'll be ready for the party?'

'Definitely.' Then, because we seemed to be straying quite a long way from my original purpose, 'I missed you at the studio, Lace. It's like, where was my entourage?!'

'Lacey didn't come to the studio with you?'

'She had netball,' I said.

'Which we won,' said Lacey.

'Well, that's good!' I said. 'Classic Lacey! You are a total winner! Hey, we should mark the occasion! What are you doing tonight? Let's celebrate!'

'Calm down,' said Lacey. 'It's not that big a deal.'

'It is. You won! You were the winning team!' I shook my invisible pompoms. 'Go, Lacey! Go, Lacey!'

'Katie, are you OK? Is Katie OK? She looks like she's having an epileptic fit.'

I looked down from the top of my imaginary cheerleading pyramid to see – oh no – Mad Jaz, who was suddenly just *there*. Maybe she'd always been there. Or maybe she'd materialized, like a sort of a demon.

She was dressed quite demonically, her school uniform accessorized with an enormous black velvet scarf and ripped lace gloves.

'I was just bigging up Lacey,' I said. 'She's the best.'

Jaz's head swivelled from me to Lacey and back again.

'The best,' I repeated. 'I cannot imagine having a better friend.'

And maybe it was my imagination or did Jaz look the tiniest bit put-out? Come to think of it, probably, it *was* my imagination. That, plus Jaz's face permanently looks a bit put-out.

'So, back to my party,' Savannah was saying. Only, Jaz wasn't listening.

'I just came over to tell you that your video has had one and a half million views.'

'Honestly,' said Lacey. 'Can we please stop talking about that stupid embarrassing video, OK? It's old news.'

'I've been thinking again about the lighting,' said Savannah.

'Not that old,' I said. 'One and a half million? That's amazing! When you think of it in terms of the population of Harltree, it's . . . loads!'

'Yup,' said Jaz. 'Bet you're glad you didn't take it down now.'

'More like, *you* didn't take it down,' said Lacey.

'Only because Katie told me not to,' said Jaz.

Oh no.

'And whether I should have different colours for different zones,' said Savannah.

'Katie asked you to take it down,' said Lacey. 'Because of how embarrassing it was for me.'

'That is the most selfish thing I have ever heard in my life,' said Jaz. 'It's lucky that she changed her mind.'

'No, she didn't. She wanted you to take it down and you said no.'

'I never said that,' said Jaz, who, to be fair, had never said that. Except in my version of events.

I was coming to realize I'd made a fairly serious error. Or, several very serious errors.

'Er, Jaz, don't you remember how I said could you take it off the internet and you said you wouldn't?' I gabbled. 'Maybe not. Oh well, moving on . . .'

'I do remember. You said you wanted it to stay up,' said Jaz.

'Did I?' I said.

'*Did you?*' said Lacey, getting to her feet. 'Because that's not what you told me. That's not what you told me at all.'

Even Savannah had stopped talking.

'You . . . lied to me,' said Lacey. 'I know you're mates with *her* now. But I can't believe you'd actually lie.'

'I never had you down as a liar, Katie,' said Savannah, looking very severe, but still pretty. 'Because if we can't believe you on this . . .'

'I'm not a liar! I mean, technically, in this particular instance, then yes, I am, but it is an absolute one-off, it really is. I mean, honestly, Lace. This is the best thing that's ever happened to me. I couldn't take it down just because you found it very slightly embarrassing. Could I? I mean, really?! Come on.'

'I just wanted the truth,' said Lacey, teetering on the edge of tears. And then going over the edge altogether.

'I'll make it up to you, Lace,' I said, as Savannah, Paige and Sofie went into a whispery cluster. 'When I get famous – which will be incredibly soon – I'll give you concert tickets, and if I get any clothes, they're all yours, as soon as I'm done with them, obviously, I mean, just because they'll probably be giving them to me for a photoshoot or a concert but if that happens I'll have them dry-cleaned, I'll do . . . whatever you want, Lacey.'

Lacey snuffled.

'Lacey, babes,' said Savannah. 'Come sit with me a moment, yes?' She patted the grass next to her.

Something about Savannah's words worked where mine hadn't. Lacey sat back down again. Now it was the four of them, in the sunshine, and me and Jaz in the shade. It couldn't have been more symbolic if it tried.

'Want to know what I'm thinking?' said Savannah.

Lacey did a little shrug.

'It'll cheer you up. Promise.'

Then Savannah said something into her ear, probably about how much of a loser I was, or that I was looking especially chubby today or something. Whatever it was, Lacey's eyes widened.

'Of course,' she said, and she did look happier. Much happier. It was kind of good but also, if I'm being honest, a bit disturbing how quickly she'd cheered up. Then, 'It's fine, Katie. And I cannot wait until your single comes out. I really can't.'

Paige smirked.

'What?' I said.

'Nothing,' said Sofie.

At which point the sun went in and the bell rang and lunchtime was over.

Oh, and on the way back inside I even saw a clump of bluebells.

CHAPTER TWENTY-FOUR

Everywhere I went, people were talking about Savannah's party. Even Mad Jaz wasn't immune.

'It's going to be the worst party anyone has ever had,' she told me as the bus fought through the morning traffic. 'Fin says that she's going to have *relatives*.'

Jaz managed to make the word 'relatives' sound like norovirus.

'So you're not going to be there tonight?'

Mad Jaz looked at me as though I was mad. 'Of course I'm going.'

'She invited you?'

'No.'

My understanding of the inner workings of Jaz was still at beginner level.

'Um, what time are you getting there?'

'Around nine.'

Nine? Nine was when I would be leaving. I tried not to let this show on my face as I said, 'OK, cool, yeah, I might be a bit earlier but not much. Late nights and pop stars don't mix.'

'Yeah they do,' said Jaz.

'Just, you know, with the single coming out and everything . . .'

Jaz did this epic sigh. 'All right, fine. Play it.'

Another corner and now we were on the fast bit of road leading up to school, where all the trees hang low over the road and three years ago a bit of the bus roof got caught on one and came off. There were pictures all over the *Harltree Gazette*. I hadn't thought about it at all since then, but I did now. Because presumably I'd be on the front of the *Harltree Gazette* again soon. I was just as newsworthy as a broken bus. Maybe even more so.

Except . . .

'They still haven't sent it to me.'

'Why not?'

'I don't know,' I said, wishing I'd had the sense to ask. 'I'm probably going in again soon, though, to talk about the album and the tour and everything. They must be waiting for that.'

'When?' Funny how, when I wanted Jaz to listen, she never would. But the very second we got into stuff that I would rather have left alone, she grabbed and hung on and wouldn't let go, like when next-door's dog got under the fence and dug up the body of Manda's hamster.

'They haven't said. Soon. It's got to be soon. At the meeting Tony said time was really important. We have to keep up the momentum. You know how it is.'

And then we were at school, or, to give its proper title, Savannah's Pre-Party Warm-Up Zone.

And if I'd had someone to get ready with later, then maybe I'd have been excited too.

Me and Lacey were so good at getting ready for parties. The getting-ready part was always the best bit, too. Having Lace do my liquid eyeliner with flicky bits coming up at the ends and me glueing fake eyelashes on to her. Trying on every last thing in whoever's house we were at, or dancing to Beyoncé in our heels and tights.

I wasn't going to let this . . . thing . . . go on any longer, I decided. Being a celebrity was a lonely business and I didn't want to end up in a humongous mansion all on my own, collecting shoes I couldn't walk in, and probably having a ton of plastic surgery because there wouldn't be anyone around to tell me I shouldn't.

I'd sort it out at the party. Whether she wanted to or not.

As it was, I did have someone to get ready with. A brown furry thing that came scuttling across the floor while I was trying to squeeze myself into Amanda's green dress. For a second I thought it was a huge spider, and then I realized it was either a mouse or a baby rat and that this was both better and also worse. Especially when I then saw a spider two minutes later, hanging next to the door.

I pulled on my sparkly tights. It certainly was quicker getting ready this way. Even the flicky eyeliner worked first time. I'd not yet got to the end of 'Single Ladies' and I was hot to trot.

Possibly it was a bit too quick; it was still only half past seven and Jaz had made it clear that arriving at a party in the first hour is literally the most embarrassing thing anyone can do. I sat back down on my bed and contemplated going downstairs for something to eat. There were definitely fish fingers in the kitchen, and I thought I remembered a punnet of eggs, too. Not quite the chocolate fountains and candy floss and personalized pizzas that the rest of my form were currently enjoying. But then, like Jaz said, you don't go to a party to eat. Or have fun.

Exactly what you *do* go to a party for, she'd not said.

I emptied my rucksack and began picking out bits to take with me: lip gloss, wallet, lipstick, tissues, tinted lip balm . . . It all just about fitted into my evening bag, which was by far the best thing I'd ever found in Harltree Oxfam: a shiny black leather purse with a proper metal chain, far too small to take anything more than basic make-up essentials, which made it completely impractical but also really lovely. I was just pushing everything else into a heap when I saw some gold writing. A piece of card. Tony's card. With his phone number on it.

And then the feeling that had been nagging me since my conversation with Jaz came creeping back.

Why hadn't Tony sent me my single? Especially when playing it at the party would absolutely sort everything out, once and for all.

All right, not quite everything.

But most of the important stuff.

Well, it would make me look cool and, really, everything else was just details.

Could I ring him, and ask for it, on a Friday night?

Bit much.

But then, this *was* an emergency.

 246

Then – of course – I knew. I wouldn't do anything stupid, like wait until Monday.

I'd send him a text!

> Hey Tony, it's Katie here. I was just wondering if my single was ready because if you could maybe send it to me I could play it at this party I'm going to tonight. Thanks! Katie xo

The reply took forever to come. Long enough to decide that the 'xo' had definitely been a mistake. Long enough for me to pluck my eyebrows, then overpluck my eyebrows, then draw them back in again with an eyebrow pencil.

Finally, when my forehead was at pretty much the limit of what it could take, I got:

> Katie, good to hear from you! Sorry, it's still being mixed at the moment. Sounds terrific though. You're going to love it. T

Well, it was something. Straight away I texted back:

> I don't mind playing whatever version you have!
>
> Also, you said I was touring soon . . . ? Where?
>
> Want to invite my friends! So excited! Kx

Another eternity, this time long enough for me to apply nail varnish and let it almost dry and then check to see if it had dried with just the lightest touch of my thumb and ruin it.

> Will be in touch about that soon. Got some great venues lined up. Madison Square Gardens. The Hollywood Bowl. And heard of a little place called Wembley?

The spider-mouse-rat finished doing whatever it had been doing down under my bed and zoomed off back across my rug.

'Mands?' I shouted. 'Mands, are you there? I have news. Manda?!'

Nothing. Just the *drip-plunk* noise of the hot-water tank filling up.

I looked in the mirror and said, over and over again, 'You are going to be a star.'

Somehow, I wasn't quite feeling it.

So here's the thing.

According to every film and TV show and every article ever, it's stupid to feel ugly and awkward at a party. Because everyone else there might *look* as though they are having a great time. They might *seem* as if they are confident and relaxed and gorgeous and happy. But actually, deep down inside, they're completely miserable and insecure and not enjoying themselves any more than you are.

I'd always been a bit suspicious of this.

And I have to say that Savannah's party proved once and for all that it is A COMPLETE LOAD OF RUBBISH.

I know this because I spent a full fifteen minutes after I arrived closely observing everyone in that tent and they were all having the most marvellous time. Ignoring me.

After an infinity of staring at Sofie's streakily self-tanned back, I gave up trying to penetrate the Savannah Circle and went and stood next to Devi Lester and his mates. He, at least, would be grateful for a little of the Katie Cox stardust.

'What?' said Devi, after about twelve hours of chat about *Star Wars*.

 249

'Nothing,' I said, going over to the food table in case there were any crisps left. Which there weren't.

There was Lacey, though, standing with the canal crowd. Wearing a purple top I'd never seen before. Had she been to Oxfam *without me*?

'. . . Helter-skelter!' she was saying. At which point everyone in the vicinity cracked up.

'Katie.'

'Hey, Lace! Ha ha!'

'Why are *you* laughing?'

'Because . . . it was funny?'

'You missed the beginning,' said Lacey, her eyes shining with a very particular kind of cruelty. 'You don't know what we were talking about.'

'Sorry,' I said, simultaneously wanting to disappear and emigrate and die. You don't point that kind of stuff out where people can hear. Especially not to your best friend. Even to your ex-best friend.

I was starting to think that this evening might have been a mistake when . . .

'Katie? This party sucks.'

Jaz was in this huge black ball dress, slashed up the legs to show all this red netting stuff, and she had about six chokers around her neck simultaneously. One was a pair of interlocking hands, which genuinely made it look like she was being strangled by her own jewellery.

'Hi, Jaz. And hi, Nicole.'

'Whoah,' said Jaz. 'That is freaking me out.'

'I know,' I said. 'I'm probably going to have nightmares about it later. Do you think you should take it off?'

'Not my necklace,' said Jaz. '*That.*'

I followed her eyes to the middle of the dance floor, where two people who I assumed were either Savannah's parents or her slaves (or, from their exhausted expressions, possibly both) were unveiling the world's most bonkers cake.

It was five tiers high, kind of like a wedding cake, if a wedding cake had been decorated so hard that it barely stayed up. Each layer was a different colour, with gold blobbles on, and flowers, and candles. And then –

'Darling, lift up your feet?' The man pulled out an extension cord, plugged it into the generator, and the whole thing lit up like Vegas as a literal waterfall started coming down from the top, *sploosh sploosh sploosh.*

It was simultaneously the best and the worst thing I'd ever seen.

'I LOVE it,' Savannah was shrieking. 'I LOVE it! I mean, it's smaller than in the picture. But I love it!'

Jaz had now made her way over to the speakers and was hooking up her phone. Ambient Karamel made way for a *bang-bang-bang* bass, overlaid with a man who sounded like he was being liquidized.

'No!' said Savannah, gliding across the floor like a seriously angry swan.

'No offence, Sav,' said Jaz, 'but your taste in music is tripe.'

'Yours is worse,' said Savannah.

'I am not staying to listen to that boy band puking up into my head.'

'Fine by me,' said Savannah.

Not quite fine by me, though, seeing as how Jaz was the only person at this party who had bothered to talk to me.

'There must be something we can all listen to,' I said, searching through her library for some Mad Jaz/Savannah crossover music. A sort of sugar-pop-metal-hardhouse fusion. Oddly enough, there didn't seem to be anything that would even slightly do.

'It's a shame you won't let us play your single,' said Jaz.

'It's literally the only thing we both want to hear.'

'You know I don't have it yet,' I said.

'So sad,' said Savannah, pityingly.

Lacey was just coming back in from the garden and even though I waved at her, she looked straight through me. As though I was a ghost. Not even the scary sort that gets to star in horror films, but the invisible kind that just trails around after proper, living people, waiting to get noticed for the rest of all eternity.

Wembley Arena, though. She'd notice me then.

But by the time I was at Wembley she'd just be a dot in the crowd. I needed her to see me *now*.

'How about I sing it live?' I said.

The canal crowd came bobbing along behind her.

'You know, unplugged. Acoustic!'

There was no time to think whether or not this was a good idea because straight away Jaz was turning off the stereo and everyone stopped talking.

A space opened up around me.

Lacey's eyes met mine and I felt myself go solid again.

This was my chance.

To show her.

To show everyone.

I opened my mouth and in my head the song swelled up behind me, a huge wave, and I let it rise, and rise, until it lifted me. And then I opened my mouth and sang.

I've got mad skin

I've got mad hair . . .

And straight away I knew I'd made a truly epic mistake.

CHAPTER TWENTY-FIVE

Basically, there was a complete disconnect between how the song sounded in my head, i.e. magical and awesome and amazing, and how it sounded in Savannah's mega-tent. Which, and I'm not going to linger on this because it is too, too painful, was not magical, or awesome, or amazing. It was small and sad and rubbish.

I got through the first bit, though, and while I missed having my guitar there every last second, I was just starting to think that maybe it would be, if not OK, then at least not suicide-level awful.

Only, then, while I was singing, I saw that Jaz was looking down at her phone, while Sofie . . . Sofie was talking.

I carried on, louder now, and shifted my eyes over to just behind Dominic Preston's gorgeous head.

And Dominic was talking too! Whispering to Devi Lester.

Aaaaaargh!

I was still going, which was my second mistake. If I'd stopped at the end of the first verse, maybe I could have saved myself, pretended I'd always meant to end there, while at least some people were still listening.

No, though. Toothpaste-for-brains Katie has to plough on like a sad slug and –

'SAVANNAH!' Paige came whizzing in. 'Karl is kissing Nicole. In your roses!'

And that was that. The whole crowd relocated itself outside to see Nicole and Karl, which, to be frank, is icky.

Still, at least I didn't have to worry about where to point my eyeballs any more, because the only person left in the disaster zone was me.

'Oh, Katie.'

And Lacey.

I stopped singing.

It was very quiet.

Except for some laughter from outside, and then a double shriek. It sounded like Savannah had chucked Karl and Nicole on to the grass. Savannah is surprisingly strong for someone who makes stick insects look pudgy.

'You poor thing.'

She came over and went to hug me. Only, because she was Lacey, she gave up at the last minute and half draped her hand on my shoulder, as though she was patting me, and I was an injured horse.

I realized that no one had put their arms around me in a while.

'That was a bit embarrassing,' I said.

'A bit?!' said Lacey, and we both laughed.

'Can we . . . can we be friends again?' I said. 'Because all this stuff is really wearing me out.'

'Me too,' said Lacey. 'It's difficult enough having to do the walk every morning on my own, without having to spend all day being upset.'

This I did not understand. 'But you're not on your own. You're with the canal crowd.'

'Who chuck my bag in the water and call me "Lacey with the stupid facey".'

'Do they?'

'They always did. And they do it even more now you're gone.'

'I thought you were all mates?'

'I have to pretend it's OK,' said Lacey, 'or I think they might chuck me in as well.' She sighed. 'I can handle the occasional dunking. But not every day. Not on my own.'

Which made perfect sense. Man, life can be hideous sometimes.

'I'm not much enjoying the bus,' I said.

'But you and Mad Jaz are total besties these days.' She said it in this flat, sad way and I felt very, very bad.

'We're friends, I suppose. Just about. Sometimes I even quite like her. I mean, she's funny, and she's exciting and she's . . .' I stopped, because this didn't seem to be going down ever so well. 'But, Lace, she's like an unexploded bomb. I just never know what she's going to do next and it's really . . .' I searched for the right word. 'Tiring.'

We had this nice moment, Lacey blinking at me from beneath her fringe, which was looking pretty good as she'd straightened it for the evening. Which I was about to tell her, when she said:

'I missed getting ready with you tonight.'

'Me too! Oh, Lacey.'

We hugged, properly this time, and it was the best of the best.

'I'm so sorry I lied about the video. I'd do anything for us to be mates again. All I want, literally, is for us to watch *Mean Girls* and have pizza. That is my complete vision of happiness right now.'

'Mine too,' said Lace.

'I need you in my life.'

'And I need you,' said Lacey. 'I hate before and after school now. They used to be my favourite bits of the day.'

'And how am I supposed to cope with all this fame stuff on my own? I need our friendship. To ground me. Otherwise I'll probably turn into one of those mental people who only eat blue M&Ms and won't let anyone make eye contact.'

'Katie, just stop.'

I was so busy thinking whether it was the blue M&Ms I'd eat, or whether the orange ones were actually better or whether M&Ms were a bit too American and it would be more patriotic to have Smarties, in which case I'd definitely go for the orange ones, that it took me a second to realize what she'd said. 'Stop what?'

'It's not that your songs aren't good. You know I like them. But all this stuff about a record label—'

'It's called Top Music.'

'Is it?' She fiddled with her zip, then looked me in the eye. And I could kind of see why some celebrities didn't like it. 'Is that really what it's called?'

'I don't understand,' I said, because I didn't.

'You don't need to pretend. Or, maybe you do, to everyone else. If you want to stay on Planet Savannah, then, OK. But don't pretend to me. Not if we're friends like you say we are.'

'Pretend what?'

'Come on, Katie. There wasn't a recording studio, was there?'

Which is when I began to realize that things were even worse than I'd thought.

'Of course there was.'

'It's OK. You've let it all go too far and it's embarrassing to admit it's made up, I know, so I'm not going to make a big thing of it. But I don't get why you need to tell all these –' and I saw her reach for the word 'lies' before stopping herself and saying – '*stories* about a label and a single and a tour and whatever. I think we'd all respect you more if you just told the truth.'

'But I did. I was.'

'It's over, Katie. You've had your five minutes and now it's done and we can all get back to normal.'

She said it so kindly. And I did think, as a series of shrieks from the other side of the canvas told me that the tent was about to fill up again, that maybe I could even go with it. I could nod, and not talk about it again, and wait until the single came out. And in the meantime we could be proper mates, like before.

But I mean, really – how could I be friends with someone who thought I was a liar?

Then there was Sofie, standing framed in lights, the garden dark behind her, shouting, 'Look! It's Harltree's number one superstar!'

And Lacey laughed.

'You don't know anything,' I said. 'You're the world's most ignorant person. You think I'd make up something like that?'

She stopped laughing, and I noticed that I was talking very loudly.

'I *have* recorded a single, a proper single in a proper recording studio. In proper London.'

'You lied about getting Jaz to take the video down. You wouldn't let me come with you to the recording. You couldn't even get Savannah her Karamel tickets. I mean, you've got literally no evidence whatsoever. Not even a photo. Why should we believe you?'

'Because –' I searched through my head – 'they had special pencils, I've got one for you, at home, and there were massive bowls of sweets everywhere and you could have as many as you wanted. And the room was this bizarre soundproofed box and there was a sort of thing over the microphone that looked like a stretched pair of tights and – how can you think I'm making this up? It's true, all of it. I recorded a single. My single.'

'Then why can't we listen to it?' said Paige.

'Because it's not out yet!' I shouted. 'There is a reason that this stuff takes a while, and you wouldn't understand because unlike me, you are not in the music industry. But there is a single and I am going on a tour, really really soon. To Madison Square Gardens. In New York.'

'Of course you are, babes,' said Savannah.

'And Wembley!' I said. Now everyone at the party was standing and staring at me, and a tiny part of my brain chose to inform me that I had the audience I wanted, just ten minutes too late. 'I am playing Wembley Arena!'

'Let it go,' said Lacey.

'Fine!' I screamed. 'I don't even care what you think. Because I don't need you! You're losers, you know that? Boring, pointless losers. And I have integrity and talent and dignity and I am taking them elsewhere.'

At which point I turned around, tripped over the extension cable and crashed straight into Savannah's stupid cake.

CHAPTER TWENTY-SIX

I've had parties end badly before. There was the time when I was seven and we all went to an ice-cream parlour and ate ten different types of ice cream, and I was sick ten different types of ice cream on the way home. Or the time I accidentally left a party in Paige's coat and then had to spend the next term trying to convince everyone I hadn't been trying to steal it.

Even so, standing outside Savannah's house, wearing her cake, for a full half-hour while I waited for Amanda to come and pick me up, was a new low.

'What?' she said, as I slid into the seat beside her, dripping gold icing all over the upholstery.

'It's nothing. I'm fine.'

Her eyes darted to take in my jacket, which was slathered with buttercream. And globs of pistachio and rose or lemon and cherry or diamond dust and unicorn tears or whatever it was that Savannah's poor team of bakers had stuck in there.

I'd eaten quite a lot while I was waiting. But that still left most of it.

'Katie, have you been . . . ?' Amanda tailed off. 'What have you been . . . ? How have you . . . ?'

'Savannah had a very large birthday cake. Until I fell into it.'

'God.' Then, 'It was an accident, I hope?'

'OF COURSE it was an accident!'

'It's just . . .'

I felt the tears start coming. 'Not you as well.'

'All right, all right, I'm not saying you did it on purpose. Don't go off on one while I'm driving, please.'

I had a go at pulling myself together, which meant singing Shania Twain lyrics in my head. I had to do the whole of 'Man! I Feel Like a Woman' and half of 'That Don't Impress Me Much' before I was calm enough to say:

'They didn't believe me. About all the Top Music stuff. They think I'm making it up.'

'Really? Even Lacey?'

'Even Lacey,' I said.

'But you've got all those hits!'

'Apparently that's not enough.'

'Well, I suppose it's understandable,' said Amanda,

finally, after we'd got through a particularly scary one-way system. 'I mean, it doesn't seem very likely, does it?'

'Why does everyone think it's so crazy that I could finally make something of my life?'

There was a long bit where we just drove in silence. By which I mean Amanda did the actual driving, but I did quite a lot of pretend steering in my head, especially when we had to go down the narrow bit at the end of the high street. Then, finally:

'You *are* making something of your life,' said Amanda. 'This is your life. Here and now. Your family and mates and school and home. We're not . . . some waiting room that you have to sit in until you finally get called into this amazing place where you think you deserve to be.'

We drove a bit more.

'They'll see when the single comes out,' I said. 'I just wish Tony would tell me when that will be. And when are we shooting the video? Or will they use the one we recorded in my room?'

Amanda made a noise that somehow told me she didn't know and also didn't care. She was probably still wrapped up in all that shop stuff.

Finally, we were at the house. I opened the car door

and there was that fresh, outside smell that I'd never had with a house before, blowing in from the trees and the fields and the sky.

And as we went up the drive I saw that the curtains weren't quite shut. There was a slice of light, and in it, I caught a glimpse of Mum and Adrian curled up on the sofa. Their faces were lit gold by whatever was on the TV, and Mum was smiling at something.

And I thought, at least I'm safe now.

I'm home.

'Katie, hey.' Adrian got up the second he saw me. 'Glad you're back early. I was just about to have some nachos. Fancy sharing?'

'Actually,' I said, 'I'm going to bed.'

'You sure?' he said. 'I'll put extra cheese on. Just the way you like them. It'll be a one-to-one ratio of nacho to cheddar.'

My stomach sent me a message to say that a load of squashed icing didn't exactly constitute dinner, so I nodded, and followed him into the kitchen. Where he shut the door with an expression that said this hadn't been about triangular crisps.

'I wanted to talk to you.'

'What about?'

'I've had Tony on the phone. Asking about this tour.'

Bubbles, bright and sparkly, came fizzing through my chest and out of my mouth in a giddy laugh. The timing could not have been more perfect!

I saw myself unrolling a poster, maybe in registration, Savannah and co. being nice, Lacey begging to be my friend again, and Jaz . . . well, I wasn't sure what Jaz would do. Hopefully something good.

'Oh my God. Oh my God! Because he talked about it at our meeting but then I didn't hear anything and I was starting to worry but this means it's all about to kick off, doesn't it? Oh my God!'

He put his finger between his eyes. 'You can't go, Katie.'

'*What?*'

'It's everything we said you wouldn't do. Foreign travel. Term-time dates.'

'So? I don't care if I miss a bit of school. I can catch up easily enough.'

'No.'

'Can't they send a tutor or something?'

 267

'Oh, and you think you'll be able to concentrate on algebra in the back of some bus?'

'I can't concentrate on it when I am at school,' I said truthfully. 'So maybe a change of venue would be helpful. Worth exploring, anyway.'

'No,' said Adrian.

'Let me just speak to Tony,' I said. 'I'm sure there's a way . . .'

'There's no point,' said Adrian. 'I told him that it wasn't going to happen.'

CHAPTER TWENTY-SEVEN

'You did what?' I said, and if it had been a film the music would have gone frightening and slow.

'I told him no can do.' His voice was completely certain, but his eyes, they were looking at the floor, the microwave, the unopened bag of nachos – anywhere, except me. 'We agreed that you would be responsible.'

I hated him, this bloke, this nobody that Mum had picked up in the pub and who was now ruining my life.

'We had a conversation about this, Katie; don't say you don't remember, because you do.'

'*You* had the conversation and *you* told me that I wasn't taking time off school. I don't remember getting a say in it.'

'You can't just go jaunting off.' His mouth had little white blobs of spit in the corners.

'You can't go telling Top Music what I will and won't do. It's not your place, OK?'

'It is exactly my place,' said Adrian. 'I'm your manager; it's what I'm here for. I'm the one looking out for you here, you've got to see that. I'm in your corner! Record labels, they pretend they're your friends, but—'

'Just because your career was a complete failure, you think mine's going to be too! Well, it's not, OK? And you are not on my side. If you were, then you'd have actually asked my opinion before you said no.' The words came tearing out of my mouth before I could stop them. 'If you were on my side, then we would have broadband! If you were on my side, then you wouldn't have dragged my sister into your pathetic failure of a so-called shop! If you were on my side, then you would leave us all alone!'

'I—'

I must have been pretty loud as in came Mum.

'What?' she said.

He glanced at me, a sad, hopeless kind of a glance.

'Nothing,' I said.

'Are you giving Adrian cheek?' said Mum.

'No,' said Adrian. 'Katie's OK. It's all OK.'

'Yeah,' I said. 'I was just . . . upset about the party.'

'Why?'

Honestly, can't a girl suffer in peace?

'I fell into a cake,' I said. Which was enough to send Mum back into the lounge.

'Katie,' said Adrian. 'Katie.'

'I am going to bed,' I said. 'Goodnight.'

'Can we talk tomorrow? We'll talk about this tomorrow!' His words followed me up the stairs, floating on a cloud of 'We're still friends, aren't we?'-ness, so I shut my bedroom door and left them bobbing about on the landing.

There had to be a way of undoing this.

If I really did have an actual tour lined up, and Adrian had only spoken to Tony a couple of hours ago, then maybe there was still time.

I got my phone out, ready for a text from Lacey, maybe, or Jaz. Or anyone.

Nothing.

Fine fine fine fine, I said to myself. I do not need them. I do not need anyone. If . . .

> Hi Tony. Heard you spoke to Adrian earlier.

I hesitated.

> Ignore him! He's just a stupid

Not ever so professional. I deleted and tried again.

> He does not have the authority to decide my schedule

A bit *too* professional. Delete.

> We got the dates muddled up. I can totally do the tour. Excited!!! Kx

I put my phone on to charge and then lay on my rug, noticing in a sort of vague way that I had stopped noticing the water stains on my ceiling.

There was something hard just under my head, its corner poking into my skull. So I reached back and flicked whatever it was across the floor.

My lyric book.

I hadn't looked at it in days. It was like seeing an old friend. By which I mean a genuine one, not a two-faced canal-buddy accuser-toad.

The pages were semi-transparent, some of them grooved by the nib of my biro, lines of ink running this way and that as the words crossed and scribbled and sometimes fought with each other and sometimes flowed, up the margins and down into corners, around the staples and jumping between lines like when me and Lacey played Ironic Hopscotch.

There were the lyrics to 'Just Me', in three different colours of pen.

And then, a blank page.

There were so many things to write about: horrible parties, renegade managers, so-called friends, miserable sisters. A billion songs' worth of stuff.

I sat up, took a pen from my desk and began . . .

Then stopped.

I tried again, the tip of my pen sitting on the paper, pouring out an inky blob. More and more blue, until the paper was wet. Until the point of the pen went straight through the page.

And still, no song.

It was all there, inside me, waiting, but for some reason, it wouldn't come out. Couldn't come through. Like I could hear the words in the distance, but whenever I tried to get close to them I smacked my face into a wall.

My phone buzzed.

> Hi Katie. That's great news but are you sure? Adrian sounded pretty certain.

Tony was there.

> Am sure.

I shut the book so those blank pages would stop staring at me.

> Can we have a quick chat? Sorry, I know it's late.

I'd barely finished reading his message before I was typing:

> Not 2 late.

The screen began to flash. I took a breath, leaned out the window and cleared my throat. Which seemed to just dislodge a hidden bit of something, meaning I had to clear it again, harder, and again, before I finally gave up and answered.

'Tony, hi!'

'Oh dear, have you got a cold?'

'No,' I said, giving my throat another small scrape and half-choking. 'I'm completely healthy. And really, I mean it about the tour. It was just a mix-up.'

'So, it's fine for you to miss school?'

'Definitely.'

'This is an issue, though,' said Tony. 'Adrian clearly doesn't want you to go. And he *is* your manager.'

'Seriously? Me saying this to you on the phone now about my life and my time doesn't count as much as something that Nose – I mean, Adrian says?'

'He's your official point of contact with us. If he says one thing and you say another . . . well, you can see that it presents us with a difficulty.'

'He shouldn't have said anything to you without talking to me first,' I said. 'In fact, I sort of think he shouldn't say anything to you at all. I didn't choose for him to be my manager. He chose himself.'

'Ah,' said Tony. 'I see. I wonder . . .' I listened to him breathing for a few moments. 'I wonder whether he's what you need, right now. You and he clearly have different ideas about the direction you need to be going in.' He paused. 'Creative differences.'

Of course.

Of course!

It was so obvious.

How come I'd not seen it until now?

'I'll get rid of him,' I said. 'He doesn't have to be my manager. Does he?'

'That's not what I was suggesting,' said Tony. 'Adrian's a mate. An old mate.' His voice crackled, and I leaned out further into the night.

'No, but that will solve this. Won't it?'

'I want to be very clear. I'm not asking you to part ways with Adrian. I just thought you could sit down and have a discussion about what you want.'

'Or, I could get rid of him and just get someone who wants what I want. And what you want. What we want!' It occurred to me that I had literally no clue how you find a manager. 'Do you know anyone?'

'We can always get you a manager, if that's what you decide.'

'Then let's do that!'

'You don't want to talk things through with him? I'm sure he has some good ideas.'

'I'm not,' I said. 'Please. Can we get him out the picture

and then I'll go on tour and everything will be like it's supposed to?'

'And we'll find someone to look after you. Good stuff, Katie. You'll tell him?'

'I will,' I said.

'Then how about you come in tomorrow for a chat?'

Which would mean skiving off. And on a guitar lesson day, too. Then again, without Adrian in the picture, it hardly mattered. 'Great,' I said. 'Around lunchtime?'

'As soon as you can get here,' said Tony, his voice so eager it was like he was reaching down the phone and pulling me on to the train. 'We have so much to talk about.'

'Yes! Sorry, I know it's silly, but I was starting to worry that . . . I don't even know what I was worrying about.'

'See you tomorrow,' said Tony.

We said goodbye to each other, and as I hung up and pulled myself back inside, I thought how much better everything was now. I had my tour, and my single. Two really good things.

Yes, I'd have to tell Adrian.

And ideally find a whole load of new friends to make up for the ones I'd lost earlier.

 277

With my duvet pulled up to my chin, and the light off so that the ceiling stains disappeared into the blackness, it really didn't seem so bad.

I'd go to London, first thing tomorrow. Momentum, that's what Tony had said I had. We'd sit down, make a plan together. Maybe he'd give me a CD to take away.

I'd come this far. Besides, in case anyone had forgotten, I had over a million hits.

It was all going to be completely fine.

CHAPTER TWENTY-EIGHT

It was a weird sort of a night, what with knowing I was about to go on this life-changing mega-tour of amazingness and then have a single come out. Every time I got excited I remembered that I sort of didn't really have any friends any more, and went a bit flat. And every time I thought about not having any friends any more, I remembered the single, and the tour, and got excited again.

So, yet another terrible night's sleep.

I was already a fingernail picker, a spot popper and a ponytail sucker; insomnia was a habit I could really do without.

I suppose I must have conked out at some point, because then the light coming through my curtains was grey and there were birds screeching, apparently right next to my head.

Living in the country is tough.

And there was a tapping noise coming from somewhere. A woodpecker, maybe. Or, a rat. Or a horse, or –

'Morning,' said Adrian. 'Can I come in?'

  279

'All right,' I said, trying to shake off dreams of crashing cakes and crazy laughter and something that I couldn't quite remember involving a levitating tractor.

'I'm sorry about last night,' he said, sitting down on the end of my rumpled bed. 'I couldn't sleep for thinking about it. And . . . I just want the best for you, you do know that?'

'I know that,' I said. Not that it helped.

'So I thought we'd go back to Top Music and say that you can tour out of term-time, if you want. And if they don't like that, we'll look for another label. And we'll talk to Zoe, be straight up with her this time, tell her all about it. We'll make it work, Katie.'

'Adrian . . .'

'Yeah?'

I focused on his massive furry feet. 'I don't think you should be my manager any more.'

He didn't say anything.

'I just reckon it'll be better for me to have someone else who's a bit more in tune with what I need. But, thank you for all your hard work. And everything.'

He stood up. 'You've decided?'

'I've already told Tony,' I said. 'So, I suppose,

280

yes. I officially have.'

What was I expecting? Probably some yelling. Definitely a lecture of some kind.

Instead, he simply got up and left.

So I suppose he didn't care that much, after all.

An hour later and I was all ready for my secret London mission.

Remembering the 'just got out of bed and not in an attractive way' look I'd been sporting last time I'd gone to Top Music, I made sure to wash and dry and brush my hair. Then I packed my grey boots with the too-high heels, a black top and my good denim skirt. Plus a lipstick I got free with a magazine, to get the look that Lacey called Big Red Mouth.

The twenty that Manda kept in her make-up bag would just cover my train fare, and I made sure to eat an especially massive breakfast as clearly there wouldn't be time for lunch. Mands gave me a bit of a look as I went for Coco Pops bowl number three, but I just ignored her.

Adrian was nowhere to be seen. Since our early morning conversation I'd been braced for the hairdryer treatment from Mum, a whole load of *What did you say*

to him? and *How dare you, young lady?* In fact, there was nothing. She just got ready for work while we listened to Florence and the Machine on the radio.

Which gave me a good chance to fine-tune my secret plan. Not that it needed much in the way of fine-tuning, seeing as how it was an awesome plan to begin with. Like all the best plans, it was daring and ambitious, and at the same time really simple and hard to mess up.

So long as the world left me to myself, I'd definitely get away with it.

Given that my current friend-count was approximately nil, it didn't seem too unfeasible.

Jaz was already at the bus stop when I got there. Funny how she had bunked off school most days for the past year until I started getting the bus, at which point she'd suddenly become Student of the Year.

I nodded in a way that I hoped she'd realize meant *please leave me alone.*

Message undelivered.

'You are nuts these days, Katie, you know that?'

Today she was wearing full school uniform, only with knee-high lace-up spike boots and her hair in a full beehive.

 282

'You're one to talk,' I said, thinking vaguely that I'd never have spoken to Jaz like that a month ago.

Her lips twitched, but I couldn't tell whether it was with laughter or something else. 'I'm not the one who kicked off at Savannah's party.'

'That was an accident.'

'Same difference.'

'Look,' I said. 'I am not you, OK? I have good reasons for what happened last night. I am about to become a pretty major celebrity and –'

She doubled over with laughter.

'What?'

'You had a tiny taste of fame,' said Jaz. 'You couldn't let it go so you're spinning out this fantasy—'

'My record deal is not a fantasy,' I said. Then, 'I didn't have you down as automatically believing what everyone else thinks.'

She liked that, I could tell. 'All right. Prove it.'

'I'm going to London today to talk to Tony Topper, who is the head of Top Music, which is a huge record label. We are going to discuss my tour and my single.'

Jaz's mouth opened like a Venus flytrap that had just finished chomping a fly and was getting ready for more.

'You're skiving to go up to London? Today?'

So much for my secret plan. 'Tell the whole universe, why don't you?'

'You think *I'm* mad,' said Jaz. 'But I've never been to London instead of going to English.'

At which, I must say, I felt a bit of pride. I'd out-Jazzed Jaz! Or, at least, I was about to.

'What time are you going, then?'

'I don't have to tell you,' I said.

'No, but you want to.'

Correct, as ever. How did she know this stuff? 'I was going to change on the bus, get off a stop early and walk to the station.'

'What time are you planning on getting there?'

'Around twelve, I suppose.'

'You'll never make it if you walk to the station. Takes way too long.'

'Does it?'

She gave me this pitying look.

'So what do I do?'

'Easy,' said Jaz. 'We'll hitchhike.'

'What?' I said. And then, as I really digested what she'd just said, '*We?*'

CHAPTER TWENTY-NINE

Honestly, I tried everything to make her go away. Which included looking awkward, having big silences fall between us, and in the end literally telling her to go away.

It was like I was speaking French or something. Not only did she not seem to understand; she also didn't seem to care. Which has always been Jaz's attitude to French, and maybe explains why her exchange partner had to go back to Paris a week early.

To start with, the hitchhiking thing was totally terrifying.

'Jaz, we mustn't. Suppose we get abducted?'

'No one would want to abduct *you*, Katie.'

Harsh. 'They might want to abduct you.'

She put her hands on her hips. 'There is no way anyone is abducting me.'

And actually, she was so scary that I kind of had to agree with her.

We went and stood down by the main road, Jaz sticking her thumb out as though she'd done this a thousand times before, and I thought: This isn't real. I really am in a film. Which then made me wonder what genre it was. Thriller? Maybe. Uplifting comedy? Probably not. Disaster movie? Definitely.

Then this silver car stopped and a man wound down the window.

'Take us to the station, yeah?'

'I'm not going that way,' said the man, by which time Jaz was already in the passenger seat.

'What are you waiting for?'

We didn't get snatched, in the end. In fact, he was quite sweet and promised he would buy my single for his god-daughter. Although as I said to Jaz, one not-murderer doesn't mean that everyone else is a not-murderer too.

By this time we were on the train, and as I finished talking, the woman opposite us said, in a loud and bossy voice:

'Shouldn't you ladies be in school?'

Jaz's reply made it very clear that she was not a lady.

Then we were at Liverpool Street and the Tube.

'Covent Garden,' I said. 'That's the Central Line and then one stop on the blue one.'

Jaz stared at me. 'You're really serious, aren't you?'

'Of course.'

'I thought you'd have given up by now.'

'Why would I do that?'

'So . . .' She couldn't have looked more surprised if I'd grown a tail. 'We're going to this music place. To talk about your tour.'

'I'm going,' I said. 'I'd really rather you didn't, though.'

'Huh,' said Jaz. 'You were telling the truth. This is going to be even better than I thought.'

The woman at reception wasn't nearly as smiley as last time, probably because Jaz had picked up a stack of magazines and was asking, 'Can I keep these?' while I said, 'It's me!'

'Who?' said the receptionist.

'Katie. Katie Cox. I'm here to see Tony Topper.'

'Is he expecting you?' said Ms Frosty.

'He said to come any time today.'

'Hold on.' She picked up her phone and dialled.

'How come she doesn't know who you are?' said Jaz. 'I thought you were their super-cool new singer.'

'I have a Katie Cox here to see you.' The receptionist nodded. 'Yes.' Then she smiled at me. 'Sixth floor.'

'Thanks,' I said. Then, to Jaz, 'See!'

The barrier opened and we stepped into a waiting lift. There was a huge mirror on one side, and I couldn't help but notice that my face was completely white with excitement. This was really and truly happening.

I pushed my hair behind my ears. Maybe Lacey had been right about me needing a fringe. No. No, she hadn't.

'Nicole? Yeah, it's important. I'm with her. In London. The music stuff, it's true. We're going in now. Tell everyone.' Jaz saw me staring and turned around from her phone. 'What?'

'Jaz, I'm skiving. It's maybe best if she doesn't tell *everyone* . . .'

Then the door opened and there was Tony.

'Katie! Come through into my office – that's right, this way . . .'

'Hi!' I looked meaningfully at Jaz so that she'd be sure to hear everything we said. 'I'm here! To talk about my tour and my new manager and my single and my album and everything.'

'Of course!' He looked *so* happy.

'Like you said, keep up the momentum!' I knew I was babbling a bit, but hopefully he hadn't noticed. He was looking at something to my left.

'I'm Jasmine,' said Jaz.

'She wanted to come,' I said, feeling like I should add something but not knowing what. 'And now, here she is.'

'Here I am,' said Jaz, her head swivelling like crazy as she took it all in, the posters, the spotlights, all that glass.

Please don't do anything, Jaz, I prayed as we sat down. *Please, behave.*

'Where's Katie, then?'

'Mmm?'

Jaz waved at the posters: Karamel enjoying their anti-gravity haircuts; Crystal Skye huddling over a piano, all eyes and shoulders, like she'd just come through a famine. 'There should be one of Katie.'

'I don't want to be on a poster,' I said, even though I quite did.

'If you say so,' said Jaz.

'Anyway,' I said, wanting to get things feeling positive, 'I told Adrian.'

Tony smiled and leaned in, looking at me with this intensity that, on anyone else, would have been slightly scary. 'What did he say? What, exactly, did he say?'

'Not a lot,' I said. 'It was fine.'

He seemed surprised. 'Really? Tell me everything.'

'I just told him that we clearly had different ideas about where I was going, and that it might be better if I was managed by someone else.'

'He must have been hurt, though,' said Tony.

'Honestly? Yes, I think he was.'

'Good,' said Tony.

'You're pretty twisted,' said Jaz.

I gave Tony a look that was supposed to say, *Jaz is so weird but don't worry, she's completely harmless.*

'So . . . my tour, then. How long do you want me to play for? And will I have a backing band because I should rehearse with them and I guess it'll have to be quite soon if I'm going off soon . . .'

'What do you want?' said Tony. He spoke slowly, carefully. Like he'd been planning it for a while. 'Tell me, Katie. Tell me exactly what it is that you want. Tell me your dream.'

'Just . . . to make good music. To connect with people. I suppose.'

'There must be more.'

'I . . . don't know.'

'Then I'll tell you,' said Tony, licking his lower lip,

staring at me, harder than ever. 'You want the whole world to hear you. You want to stand on a stage and play to millions. You want the house and the pool and the cars. You want the girls screaming your name. You want it all.'

'Girls?' said Jaz.

Tony's eyes bored into mine. 'You want it all.'

'Maybe.'

'Say it. Say "I want it all."'

'I . . . I want it all.'

'Louder.'

'I WANT IT ALL.'

'And you'll never have any of it.'

'Um, what?'

'Remember this feeling, Katie. Because I want you to tell him. I want him to see it in your eyes.'

'What's going on?' said Jaz.

And Tony said, 'There will be no single. There will be no album. There will be no tour.'

'But we recorded . . . You said . . . We agreed . . .'

'How does it feel?' said Tony. 'How does it feel to be on the brink of something and have it snatched away?'

And then I knew, and it felt like falling, down, down, down. 'You can't,' I said. 'This isn't . . . right.'

'What is going on?' repeated Jaz.

Tony smiled at her as though she'd asked him for the time. 'Many years ago, I was in a band. We recorded a single. We were going to make it very big indeed. But before we could, someone split us up.'

'But you said . . . you forgave him!' I stuttered. 'You said it was all OK!'

'Did I ever say that?' said Tony. 'Did I ever say it was "*all OK*"?'

And I could see that it really, really wasn't.

My heart was fluttering around in my chest like a trapped hummingbird. Because if there was no single, no tour, no nothing, then what would I tell Lacey? What would I do?

And what had I done?

'I'm not him,' I pleaded. 'You can't . . . you can't punish me just because . . . You can't!'

'You will tell him, won't you? How he ruined your life? I hope you will,' said Tony, the base of his neck flushing ham-pink. 'We were *right there*, Katie. The whole nation was going to see us, and he walks out without a care in the world. Well, this time, this time he'll care.'

'He still cares!' I said. 'For your information, he's still

upset about it now, like, a billion years later!'

'It was *one song*,' said Tony. 'It was pre-recorded. All he had to do was stand there and mime. But we're in the studio and the audience are sitting down and the lights come on and suddenly he's all, "What are we doing, Tony?" and, "Are we losing our way?" and, "We're a live band, not puppets," and then he's asking why we were there, what music is really for. And so I told him. It's for making money! And we were about to make more money than we'd ever dreamed of. And then . . . he just walks off the set.'

'I'm glad he did!' I said. 'Imagine if he'd spent the rest of his life with *you*!'

That got him. The hairy bit between his open collar turned the colour of minced beef. 'That useless piece of . . . What's he made of himself? Nothing! Just some pointless little shop in the middle of nowhere, never married, beer gut like a—'

'LEAVE HIM ALONE,' I screamed.

'Oh, now I will,' said Tony, suddenly calm as anything again. He picked up a phone. 'Security?'

'But . . . he said you were old friends, he was at your wedding . . .'

 293

'Yeah,' said Tony, as two men in dark jackets appeared behind the glass doors.

'It's my song. You can't just—' Then one of the men had his arm around my shoulder.

'Come on,' said the security guy.

'Tony,' I shouted. Then, to the security guard, 'Get OFF ME. Tony? Tony!'

He was standing, watching me, his arms folded.

'Take it easy,' said the security guy. 'Let's get you downstairs.'

So I turned around. Which was a real shame, as I missed Jaz throwing a vase of flowers into Tony's face.

And then we were back outside, with the rest of Covent Garden carrying on as if no one's life had been ruined.

Jaz checked her watch. 'It's still early,' she said. 'Let's go nick stuff from Zara.'

I was scrolling through the contacts on my phone, up and down, up and down. Not Amanda, I'd only get a lecture, and not Mum, no no. Not Dad, either – he'd probably start telling me the latest on Catriona's Pilates studio.

I went right the way around until I got back to 'A'.

Adrian.

Adrian would sort it out.

He was on my side, he'd know what to do . . .

Only, his phone went straight to voicemail. I went to redial, and as I did, saw I had a text from Amanda.

WHERE R U??????????????? Skool called.

R U really in LDN????!

And Mum found out bout record deal.

My hands were shaking as I typed my reply.

Record deal is off. R u with Adrian?

Need 2 speak 2 him ASAP.

A second, standing outside the Tube, with all of London whirling on by, and then:

Mum and Adrian split up.

CHAPTER THIRTY

So I'd got my wish.

Adrian was out of my life.

The house would go too, I guessed, what with it being half his. Another home gone. The third one in a year. Surely some kind of record.

I was face down on my bed when Mum came in. If she'd noticed I wasn't in my uniform, she didn't say so.

'Katie, love, please don't cry.'

'Mum,' I said. 'Oh, Mum.' My head found its way on to her shoulder, smelling that familiar mix of the special washing powder she uses for her uniform and Elnett hairspray.

'We're better off without him,' she said.

'Are we?' I couldn't see her face, but I felt her body go stiff.

'A man like that . . .'

'Like what?'

'Forcing you into a career to make up for his own failures . . .'

 296

'It wasn't . . .'

'Knowing you weren't sure, knowing I didn't want you to have any part in this. And then, when I confronted him, you know what he said?'

'. . . No . . .'

'He told me he couldn't do "family stuff". That he'd come to it too late in life. That he'd tried and tried and he knew you'd never accept him. Where did that even come from? Sounds like a coward's way out to me. Which I told him.'

Or, I thought, the perfectly natural reaction of someone who'd just been informed by his potential stepdaughter to leave her family alone.

And he'd been right about Top Music. He'd been right all along.

'Mum,' I said. 'It's not . . . it's not just him. I wanted to do the record label stuff.'

'But he pushed you—'

'I pushed him.'

'He lied to me—'

'I made him lie.'

She drew back. 'How?'

'By . . . by saying that I'd start being nice to him. He was so desperate for us to be friends. And . . . and . . . we were, we were hanging out and going to London together. Only then, last night, I was horrible. I said some bad stuff.'

Mum was standing away from me now. 'What did you say?'

'I told him to get out of my life. But that was only because he'd been telling this record label that I wouldn't go on tour in school time—'

'Of course you're not going on tour in school time.'

'And he kept saying that something was wrong. And he was right! He was completely right and I should have listened to him but I didn't.'

I was crying all over again now, but this time it was clear that there'd be no more hugs from Mum. Not now, maybe not ever.

'So you're telling me that Adrian is not the villain here. That the villain is you.'

I nodded, and sobbed.

'That you forced him to go against my will, against his own better judgement, just so that you could get what you wanted.'

More nod-sobs.

'That a good man came into our lives and you,

Katie Cox, drove him away.'

I raised my head and looked into Mum's eyes. And, oh God. What had I done?

She turned to go, unhappiness sort of swirling around her in an invisible cloak. Then, 'We have broadband again. He said to tell you. Insisted, in fact. The man can't afford a new pair of shoes, but he got you back online. The password –' and she hesitated, just for a second – 'the password is "superstar".'

It took a while before I was anything like together enough to open up my laptop.

But then, eventually, I did, and there was 'Just Me'. With two million, one hundred and seventy-three thousand views, and pages and pages and pages of comments.

Need MORE

Cant live without her

Feels shes like 1of us ☺

yes!!!!!!!!!!!!!!!!!!

Do u think shes 4real???

yes!!!!!!!!!!!!!!!!!!!

She is true. That's why I ♥ her

me 2. Katie u rock!

This went on and on and on. I read how brave I'd been to show everyone my bedroom. How my lyrics were honest and how you could really see that I was close to my family and my friends. That they'd wanted someone who was good and real. How that someone was me.

If I'd been feeling bad before I'd logged in, well, now, I felt like I'd gone through bad and out the other side into a new place where bad was actually quite good.

Back at the top of the page, Past Katie was singing, as though nothing had happened.

When everything had happened.

I reached for a tissue, because, you know, unhappiness makes for mucus, and managed to knock the box down the side of my bed. A quick flail for it and I put my hand smack bang into the middle of that old pizza, which by now was doing something really interesting, and which also meant I needed a tissue even more. So I got down and reached properly, and my hand closed on the corner of something hard.

Only, it wasn't the tissues. It was the little box Lacey had given me on our last walk together.

Very carefully so as to avoid smearing it with pizza slime, I opened it. On the top, a pair of Magnum sticks, tied together with a bit of ribbon.

And then I knew what I had to do.

What I wished I'd done in the first place.

I took a deep breath.

And then I texted Jaz.

> Please take the video down. It's all over. K x

I shut the laptop and turned off my phone.

It was so still, and the house was so quiet. A light rain was falling from a heavy grey sky, more mist than droplets. What would I do now? What *could* I do?

And then I looked across my bedroom and saw.

Propped up behind my door, like it had been waiting for me to notice it, was my guitar.

CHAPTER THIRTY-ONE

What did Amy Winehouse do when she split up with her husband? She wrote 'Back To Black'. When Dolly Parton's bloke started messing around with this girl who worked in his bank, she wrote 'Jolene'. And when Morrissey was upset, he wrote pretty much all the stuff he's ever done.

What I'm saying is that there's a rich history of miserable people writing really amazing music.

Not that my music was anything even close to amazing. Now that the Top Music fantasy had gone, I could see that. All the dreams about Wembley and the single, they'd melted away like snow in the sun, and I don't know how I'd ever thought any of it was real. No way was I a star, or anything like one. I was just some spotty schoolgirl who liked to play and sing. Savannah, Paige and Sofie knew it. Lacey knew it. And now I did, too. I wasn't the next Amy Winehouse. I wasn't even the next Crystal Skye.

But I certainly had enough heartbreak to join the club.

I picked up my guitar and it fitted so nicely under my

arm, a missing piece of the Katie jigsaw. Then I flicked open my lyric book with my other hand and wrote:

I was wrong. So wrong
Wrong about my life
Wrong about my song

Then I sang it, and let the notes work themselves free, feeling the music ripple from under me, the hard catch of the strings and the way they bit into my fingers. My calluses were going. How long since I'd practised?

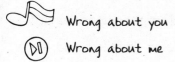

Wrong about you
Wrong about me

And so I sang, and scribbled, and played, as outside the street lights came on and the world kept turning. Until it was finished, and I knew where I had to go, and what I had to do.

Harltree high street is not somewhere you want to be after dark. What with clubbers staggering in and out of Heaven, and the kids that sit on the steps by McDonald's, it's all pretty edgy. Like, OK, no one's got a gun or anything, but you can do some pretty serious damage with a bottle of Smirnoff Ice.

As I passed the main group a girl was screaming something, and for a second, I considered getting myself safely back home again. Then I saw that it was Nicole, fighting with another girl over a shoe.

Deciding that more information would not necessarily make me feel better, I picked up the pace, until I was off the high street, down past the shopping centre and on to the row of charity shops and places selling bits of Tupperware and cheap wrapping paper.

Vox Vinyl was the last one before the shops ran out altogether, and the shutter was down. I'd failed. I . . .

No, there it was, along the pavement: a needle-thin sliver of yellow.

I thumped on the cold metal, once, twice, thrice, whatever the word for four times is, and I shouted, 'HEY. IT'S ME. OPEN UP.'

After a couple of minutes I heard a shuffling, and then about thirty different bolts sliding open before the shutter *thunk-click*ed upward, and Adrian was unlocking the door.

What I saw was so surprising that I actually forgot why I'd come.

Because it was just lovely in there. Every last inch of the wall was covered in posters, and fairy lights were strung around a little wooden platform, stacked high with shelf upon shelf of vintage vinyl. The record racks were labelled with these awesome fluorescent signs that said things like *GROOVE IS IN THE HEART* and *DANCE BABY DANCE* and *IN THE HOUSE*, and someone had done a huge mural on this monster speaker, of instruments and microphones and notes and hearts all twined together.

It was cosy and it was cool.

Vox Vinyl was *ace*.

He watched me stare. 'Your sister did all this. We were just this scuzzy record shop before, but she's completely transformed the place. Look at that!' He waved at the fairy lights. 'She's even made a little stage so we can do live stuff!'

'I bet everyone loves it.'

'I'm sure they would. If they just knew about it.'

A clubber staggered past, chucked out of Heaven and by the sound of it on his way down to hell.

'Come through to the back,' said Adrian. 'I'll make you a cup of tea.'

I followed him through a door behind the counter and into what must normally have been the stockroom. Not tonight, though. Tonight, the boxes had been shoved to one side to make room for a drum kit, stacked precariously in the corner, a keyboard, a couple of guitars and on the tiny bit of floor that was left, a lilo and our spare duvet. The one used by Auntie Jean's dog.

'Can't really afford a hotel,' said Adrian. 'Thought I'd sell my instruments to tide me over, but no one wants them. I've made a bit of a mess of it all, really.'

Hearing him say it just made things worse.

'*I've* made the mess,' I said, hearing how lost I sounded. 'You were totally right about Tony. He didn't want to make me a star. He just wanted revenge on you.'

Adrian had been looking pretty bad to start with. This didn't help. 'The old – Oh, Katie. Katie, I'm so sorry.'

'And now my music career is over. And I don't care, really, only I've made Manda hate me and I've lost all my friends and . . .'

Credit where it's due, he didn't put his arm around me and he didn't tell me it was OK. He made some tea, and then listened while I told him about the conversation in the office and Jaz tipping a vase of flowers over Tony's head.

'Good for her.'

'Yeah,' I said, smiling at the memory of Tony blinking bits of wet leaf from his eyelashes. 'I sort of wish I'd done it.'

We both laughed.

'Are you sure you don't care about a music career?' said Adrian. 'If I was you, I'd be pretty upset.'

'No. Not really. I mean, I get scared when I sing to more than three people at a time and I haven't done any proper playing in ages. No. I'm glad it's over. I'm glad the video's gone and I don't want to go on tour. It's a relief, really. I'll just go back to school and forget this ever happened and—'

And then I surprised myself by bursting into tears.

'What?'

'It's just . . . it was *my* song. And people liked it . . . And I was so proud. And now it's ruined.'

'Are you sure?'

I thought of everything that had happened. 'Yeah,' I said. 'I'm sure.'

 307

'Well. You'll write more.'

'I suppose so.'

Somewhere upstairs, a toilet flushed. And outside another set of clubbers staggered off to find the taxi rank.

'You'll have more chances.'

'And so will you,' I said.

He laughed, in that way people do when something is the opposite of funny.

'I mean it,' I said.

'I don't think so,' said Adrian. And from the way he spoke I could tell we weren't just talking about his music.

If I'd felt bad when I arrived, well, now I felt bad times one hundred. Times one thousand.

I'd had lots of worst moments recently. This, though, this was the worst of worst. It was even worse than that encounter with Mum, which is mental, because she was Mum and he was just Adrian. Adrian, who had a creaky leather jacket and hairs coming out of his nose.

It was worse because at least, when all this was over, Mum would have me and Amanda.

Adrian wouldn't have anyone.

'I'm sorry,' I said. 'If it wasn't for me, you and

Mum would still be together.'

He did this little twitch. The very tininess of it showed me just how much it hurt.

'I should never have made us go to Top Music behind Mum's back. I knew it would drive her bananas, and I did it anyway.'

'But I let you,' said Adrian.

'Still,' I said. 'It really was my fault. And I know you won't be able to forgive me. But at least . . . at least I've said it.'

He was smiling, very slightly. 'I can forgive you.'

'I don't deserve it.'

'Probably not. But I'll do it anyway.'

The fairy lights shone and suddenly it was like Christmas. Hope was swooping through me like birds, and if we'd been in a film the soundtrack would have been rising as I said:

'I've talked to Mum already; she knows it was me. She's pretty narked at the moment, but she'll get over it. At some point.' I knew I was babbling, but honestly, I couldn't help it. 'So, if you really can forgive me, and if Mum understands that this was really nothing to do with you, then . . . then . . .'

'Then what?'

'Then you and Mum can sort things out,' I said.

He put his head in his hands. 'I don't know.'

'But it's way obvious! You should be together!'

His face told me that maybe the soundtrack wasn't rising in hope, but had faded into sad, slow chords, falling like the misty rain. 'Your mum and me . . . we're not some loose end to be tied up, just like that.' He stared at me over the edge of the mug, dark hairs curling over those thick fingers, his chin prickling with specks of black, and of grey. 'I'm not an idiot, Katie. I know you think I haven't noticed you rolling your eyes at me and telling your friends that you can't stand me.'

'No . . . ' I began.

'I've lived alone my whole life. I liked it. Doing my own thing, you know? Everyone paired up except me, and for a while I wondered what I'd done wrong. And then they started divorcing again, and I realized I was well out of it. Always thought I'd stay out, until your mum turned up. And it was good, for a while. But it's difficult, being in a family. Especially when that family's not yours.'

'I'm sorry,' I said, for about the billionth time.

'It's not your fault,' said Adrian, sounding very, very

 310

tired. 'But it is . . . hard. And it's late. You should be getting home. I'll call you a cab.'

'You're not coming too, then?' I said, hopelessly.

'Not tonight, no. Maybe I'm not supposed to be happy. Maybe Tony was right.'

It was then, as I was going back through the shop, that I noticed the sign behind the counter. The sign that said *CLOSING DOWN*.

And all the other signs saying things like *BUY ONE, GET ONE FREE* and *EVERYTHING MUST GO*, which is also the name of an album by the Manic Street Preachers that I'd been meaning to get. Adrian was probably selling it off cheap, but somehow I didn't feel like asking.

He saw me take it in. 'Yeah. Gonna shut the doors on Thursday. Bank account's empty.'

'But . . . I'll tell people at school to come, everyone loves a bargain, and maybe you could do one of those gigs Amanda was talking about, or . . .'

'Katie, I don't want to do this any more. Any of it.'

And that was that.

CHAPTER THIRTY-TWO

What could I do?

I wrote.

I wrote and I played and I played and I wrote.

When I wasn't with my guitar, time ran slow and it was like even the air hated me. It was only the music that made things, if not OK, if not even bearable, then kind of maybe existable. Maybe.

I played from when I woke up until it was time for breakfast, spreading my toast with sore fingers, and it didn't matter when no one spoke to me in lessons because the songs were talking in my head. My phone stayed switched off and my curtains were drawn and if anyone was worried, they didn't mention it. Probably they didn't even care. Amanda sat with Mum in the kitchen until late every night, but I don't know what they were talking about as every time I came close they went quiet. And in the mornings we all three moved through the house like ghosts.

'Aren't you going to work today?' I asked Mands,

finding her slumped over the kitchen table, stirring some Weetabix sludge around and around and around.

'I don't think it would be appropriate. Do you?'

'I don't know,' I said.

'And anyway, even if it was, it's too late. The shop's finished.'

'It's not! I saw how cool you'd made it in there. You've done amazing things. I bet if you went back in this week and did a really big push, you could get people in, turn it all around . . .'

'Too late,' said Amanda, more to herself than to me. 'Too late.'

You wouldn't have known anything was wrong with Mum, not unless you knew what to look for. She was like a TV that had been set up very slightly wrong, her eyes too dark and her smile too bright. Her expressions didn't stay on her face but sort of twitched across it like she couldn't bear to hold the emotion for more than a second or two. I'd seen her like this before, in those weeks after the divorce. I did not want to see her like that ever again.

And me? I couldn't shake off the feeling that I'd been given something rare and special and that I'd thrown it away. As if they'd discovered one last dodo in the world at the exact moment I was eating it for dinner.

So I wrote about it. I wrote about everything. Mum, Manda and Adrian. I wrote about how alone I was, at home, on the bus, in Art when we had to get into groups and everyone had someone except me.

If living was difficult, the writing was easy. All those words and notes came rushing up to the surface, like the fat goldfish in the school pond, until my lyric book was full and I was writing in Manda's old address books and on Mum's bank statements and on the back of the wallpaper that had flaked off in the hall.

'I want to apologize for trashing your cake,' I told Savannah. 'It was an accident. But I'm really sorry. And I know I basically shouldn't have shouted. It was a disrespectful thing to do.'

'Babes,' said Savannah, 'it's fine.'

Was she saying she'd forgiven me? 'Are you saying you forgive me?' I asked.

'Meh,' said Savannah, as though there was a patch of sticky stuff on the table in front of her, and she'd accidentally put her hand into it, and the sticky stuff was me. 'Katie, you are so not even on my radar right now.'

Lacey wasn't much better.

'I've, um, look, I know that I've sort of been a bad friend,' I told her, having got the early bus so that I could catch her as she came across the field.

'Yup,' said Lacey.

'Screaming at you was way out of order. I do care what you think.'

'OK,' said Lacey.

'So, look, can we be mates again?'

Lacey stopped to think about it, the wind ruffling her fringe. 'The thing is, Katie, all we've done since you got the bus is fight. And I don't want that any more. So, yes, we can be not-enemies. But it's just easier for me if you do your thing and I do mine.'

It was as though some invisible wall had come down between me and the rest of the world. And whatever I said, the words wouldn't get across. Like words weren't enough.

'Yeah, well,' said Jaz when I told her, in PE, supposedly fielding during rounders. Only, I was so toxic these days that even the ball avoided me. 'Anyone can say anything. McAllister can fly. I'm the president of China. You have a weird nose.'

'Do I?'

'The point being, whatever,' said Jaz. 'Why should they care what comes out of your mouth? Why should anyone?'

Sometimes Jaz really bleaks me out.

'I just wish Lacey would understand,' I said, watching as, in the far distance, Sofie chopped at the ball and then ran smack into Devi Lester. 'If she could just hear how I feel, she might get a tiny part of what's in my head. I've been writing all these songs and she'll never listen to them.'

'Why not?'

'Jaz,' I said. 'You were at Savannah's party. I am not just going to whip my guitar out and start serenading her in the middle of Maths. There is a time and a place for that kind of thing.'

'Where?' said Jaz. 'And when? I want to be there.'

'Um, that would be never,' I said.

Lacey was standing in the batting queue now, laughing at something Kai was saying, then bending down to tie up her shoelace, all the time being careful never to look at me.

And then I knew.

I had to sing to her.

Because singing is what I do.

Only, there was no way I'd be doing another bedroom concert. And singing at parties, Savannah's or otherwise, was out of the question.

What I needed, I realized, was somewhere intimate. The kind of place where people would respect the music. Where they would actually hear me.

Somewhere a little bit romantic. A little bit special.

Somewhere like that little wooden platform in Vox Vinyl, all strung with fairy lights.

Only, it was closing on Thursday.

And Thursday was today.

'Jaz, I have to do a gig.'

She laughed. 'You really don't know when to stop, do you?'

Maybe not. 'Listen, I know it's mad and I'll look like a berk. I just think that maybe this is my last chance to, well, not make everything OK, but slightly less awful.'

'When?'

'Tonight.'

'What?!'

'I know! There's no time, but the shop's going to be

 317

closed tomorrow. Adrian will go away. It's my last chance.'

I thought through what I'd have to do. Get Mum and Adrian and Mands and Lacey into the room together and keep them there long enough to get through just a few songs, songs like 'Sorry' and 'Autocorrect' and 'Song for a Broken Phone'.

'You want to arrange a gig for tonight?' said Jaz. 'In the shop of a guy who has decided he doesn't want anything to do with you any more? And you're going to invite your mum, who's split up with him and doesn't want to see him, and your sister, who doesn't want to see you?'

'And Lacey,' I said, watching her swing her bat, and miss. 'Who hates me.'

'You'll never manage it,' said Jaz.

'Thanks for the pep talk.'

'. . . without me.'

After all the surprising things that had happened, this was perhaps the most surprising. A million people watching my song, I could get my head around. But Jaz wanting to help?

It just goes to show that life is a journey which takes you to some very unexpected places.

'You're really saying that you can get Mum and Adrian

and Amanda and Lacey into the shop to hear me sing?'

'If you give me their numbers.'

Which, under any normal circumstances, would have been complete madness.

Only, I was starting to think that maybe something had changed. I'd gone so far down, there wasn't really anywhere left to sink to, but there was Jaz, still at my side.

I handed her my phone. 'Here.'

'Am I allowed to lie?' said Jaz.

'No! Well, maybe. Only a little bit.' I had one more think. 'Just . . . don't say anyone's dead.'

'You are no fun,' said Jaz.

After that, I couldn't eat. I couldn't drink, either, for a bit, only then my throat got really dry and I found I could.

Mainly, though, I couldn't practise.

Knowing I was about to play to all the people I loved most in the entire world froze my fingers and made my voice go froggy. After three attempts at 'Sorry' I gave up, and opened my laptop and put in my name.

And the video was gone.

It really was over.

One minute, a million hits. The next, nothing.

I tested out the feeling, like you do with your tongue after you lose a tooth. And . . . it was all right. Honestly, it was. A bit painful, yes. But liveable-with. Unlike some other stuff.

I noticed the clock in the corner of the screen. I'd told Jaz to have everyone there for seven o'clock. Which was in less than an hour.

No time to brush my hair or put some make-up on or for any of the things I'd been planning to do. Well, the people who'd be watching had all seen me without my eyeliner. They'd seen me wearing a cake. They wouldn't care.

If they even came.

I slung my guitar on to my back.

6.25 p.m. If I was going to leave, it would have to be now.

'You can do this, Katie,' I said.

Even though I really wasn't sure I could.

CHAPTER THIRTY-THREE

The first person I saw was Adrian, unlocking the shop door with this look of complete terror on his face. His hands must have been shaking because he dropped his keys. Twice.

Then Mands came racing around the corner like she was in the sea and someone had shouted 'Shark!'

'Are you OK?' she panted. 'Adrian, ARE YOU OK?'

'I don't know; I'm not in yet.' Adrian rattled at the door. 'Come *on*!' Then he was inside and turning frantic circles. 'Where is it?'

'What?'

'The fire. There's a fire in the shop. The shop is on fire.'

'No it isn't,' said Amanda. 'But look, I need to get you to a hospital, all right?'

'Not even any smoke,' said Adrian.

'Just come with me and everything will be all right,' said Amanda.

'What . . . Why?'

'I had a text from Katie saying you'd tried to throw yourself into the river.'

'I haven't tried to throw myself into the river.'

Amanda stood back and looked at him. 'Are you sure? Not even a bit?'

'I'm sure. Really. I'm not the happiest guy in the world right now, but I'm not that bad.'

'That is the last time I give my phone to Jaz,' I said.

'AMANDA!' Mum's car screeched on to the pavement and she was out of it before the engine even stopped running. 'Don't you even THINK about it.'

'About what?'

'It's been a difficult few days,' said Mum, 'and we're all very tense, but I promise, getting a tattoo will not help. Especially not of a dragon. Especially not ON YOUR FACE.'

'I'm not getting a tattoo,' said Amanda. 'Er, Katie, would you mind telling us what's going on?'

We went into the shop, everyone still a bit shaken, to be honest, and then they looked at me.

'I'm sorry about . . . all . . . that,' I said. 'I just needed to get you here and I knew you wouldn't want to come.'

Mum and Adrian exchanged a glance, a glance that could have been the complete definition of the word 'awkward'.

'Why?' said Amanda.

This was so embarrassing. 'Because,' I said, my cheeks as hot as magma, 'I sort of have some stuff I'd like to play you.'

'Really?' said Mum. 'You really think that—'

'I know,' I said. 'But look. You're here now. It'll only take a few minutes. Promise me you'll stay and listen, just for a bit? And then we can all go home and pretend this never happened, if that's what you want.'

Mum looked like she was ready to start pretending now, but, good on him, Adrian pulled back the record racks and unfolded a few chairs, while Manda switched on the fairy lights and made everyone some coffee. And said, again and again and again, that there really was no way she'd ever get a tattoo. Which wasn't entirely true: I knew she actually had a teensy little rose on her back, which she'd had done when she went to Ibiza.

So while that was happening I tuned my guitar, probably taking a bit longer than was strictly necessary, then shuffled my chair into every possible position you can have a chair on a small wooden platform.

At which point Mum and Adrian and Mands were sitting, waiting.

'Right,' I said. 'I'm ready now.'

Was I ready? Was it about to be Savannah's party all over again? At least there weren't any cakes for me to destroy.

I cleared my throat.

'OK,' I said. 'I've been doing a lot of thinking lately. And a lot of writing. And I reckon that the best way to show you what I've come up with is to sing. This first one's called "Sorry". And I really, really mean it.'

I let the first chord trickle out from beneath my fingertips.

I was wrong. So wrong.
Wrong about my life
Wrong about my song

As I sang, Jaz slipped through the door of the shop and gave me a big thumbs up.

Wrong about you
Wrong about me
All I can say
Is sorry

That first song went by in a complete blur. I don't know where I looked, or whether anyone was listening. All I know is that I've never meant anything more. I didn't even notice that I'd finished until they started to clap.

'Um, so that's the first one. The next one is . . . oh. Hey, Sofie.'

Sofie, Paige and Savannah had come in and were sitting down on the floor. And Dominic Preston, who was managing to be more good-looking than ever.

Aaaaaargh!

I glanced over at Jaz, who just grinned.

'The next one is . . . ?' said Mum. Which meant she wasn't about to leave. At least not for another song, anyway.

I swallowed. 'The next one's called "Autocorrect",' I said.

And now, now it was starting to feel like maybe I wasn't going to crash and burn, even when the door opened again, and Devi Lester came in, and then Finlay, holding up their phones and swaying the screens in time with the beat.

So I sang. I sang to them all. I sang all the stuff that I'd only ever admitted to my lyric book; stuff that I'd have thought would make them laugh and hate me. Which perhaps it would, later, or tomorrow.

But while I kept singing, they kept listening and clapping, and more people came, some year sevens from the bus, my guitar teacher Jill, Cindy from Cindy's, even – oh Lord – even McAllister was there, and the Head, crowding in at the back, both wearing jeans. I don't know what was more surprising: that they'd turned up, or that they knew how to dress casual.

Finally, when the shop was full to bursting, I said:

'Why did you come?'

A silence. Then someone shouted, 'Jaz!' and there was a lot of giggling.

'Oh no. What terrible awful hideous thing did she say to get you here?'

'She said that you'd be spilling up your guts live in concert,' said Sofie. 'And that we had to tell everyone we knew.'

Ah. Yes, that would do it.

Then, from Jaz, right at the front, 'Why are *you* here, Katie?'

All those faces, open and waiting, lit in smudges from the fairy lights and phones.

'To say . . . to say that I was an idiot. This guy from Top Music, Tony, he told me he would release "Just Me" as a single. He said I'd be going on tour. That I'd have everything I wanted. Everything I thought I wanted. And I believed him . . . which was stupid. Because I've got everything I want here.' My voice went a bit funny. 'Do you mind if I take a quick break? Is that OK?'

Everyone said that it was, and so I stopped, and staggered into the stockroom on legs of jelly.

Mum and Adrian followed, as Mands called, 'Is it all right if I open up the till? People seem to want to buy things.'

I sank down on to a box as Mum said, 'Katie, that song. "Autocorrect".'

'Er.' My eyes slid away. 'Sorry. I . . . '

'Is that really how you've been feeling?'

'No!' Then I remembered why I was here. 'I mean, yes.'

Mum's face did something quite complicated, and then, completely unexpectedly, she pulled me into a hug.

'It's OK,' I told her shoulder.

'It isn't,' said Mum. 'But we'll work on it.'

We pulled apart, and I saw her eyes focus in on something behind me.

'Adrian, have you been sleeping in here?'

'Just a few nights,' said Adrian.

'On this?' She pointed at the lilo.

'Yeah,' said Adrian.

'I thought you'd be in a hotel.' As she said it, Mum leaned on the stack that was Adrian's drum kit. Which fell down, making exactly as much noise as you'd expect.

'Bit expensive,' said Adrian quietly.

'So why didn't you go and stay with Neil? Or your mum? Someone in the pub must have a spare room.'

He rubbed at his cheek. 'Wasn't really thinking straight.'

We might have gone on like this for a while, as Mum hadn't even got as far as finding out where Adrian was cleaning his teeth, only Jaz came shoving in.

'It's gone mad out there.'

'I know. McAllister? At my private gig? What were you thinking? And, how did you even know her number?'

'You haven't noticed?' said Jaz. Then, to the world at large, 'She hasn't noticed!'

'Noticed what?! Jaz, you are making me crazy!'

In answer, Jaz took my hand and dragged me back into the shop, where Amanda appeared to be selling every record she had.

'Look,' she said.

'What? What am I supposed to be seeing?'

'Outside,' said Jaz.

I focused on what was behind the glass. And then . . . then I saw.

People. People pressed up against the window with their phones held high, not just a few, but rows and rows and rows, so that every inch of the glass was filled, like we were in a zombie movie, only scarier. They saw me and began to wave and shout.

'Who are they?' I whispered.

'There's more of them,' said Jaz. 'I just looked down the street. They're everywhere.'

I darted back into the stockroom and sat down on the floor until the world stopped spinning, only it wouldn't stop but just went faster and faster.

'How do they know you're here?' said Adrian. 'I don't know how news can travel so quickly.'

I knew.

Oh yes, I knew all too well. I don't know why I hadn't thought of it sooner.

'Um, Jaz. The people holding up their phones. Were they . . . putting this online?'

 329

She nodded.

'And . . . ' I said, slightly not wanting to know the answer, 'are there people . . . out there . . . on the internet . . . watching?'

Jaz nodded again. And as she did so, I heard a chant begin.

'KA-TIE. KA-TIE. KA-TIE.'

'Better go and do the second half,' said Adrian.

'But . . . I can't,' I said. 'This was supposed to be just us. Now it's everyone. Everyone except . . .'

'Except who?' said Mum.

'Except Lacey,' I whispered.

'I did try to get her here,' said Jaz, looking surprisingly defensive. 'Even though she's an annoying drip with stupid hair. I did try.'

Which gave me an idea. 'I've got one more chance,' I said. 'Give me my phone.' And then I texted:

> Hey Lace. We're not friends anymore and I get it.
> I don't deserve u. But look, can u get to Vox Vinyl ASAP?
> This is the last thing I'll eva ask, I promise. I need u 2 cut
> me a fringe.

'That'll do it?' said Jaz, looking over my shoulder.

'KA-TIE. KA-TIE. KA-TIE.'

'I don't know,' I said. 'Come on. I'd better finish this.'

She didn't come. I sang 'Cake Boyfriend' and 'Honour Your Waist' and 'London Yeah' and 'Mobility Scooting on the Pavement'. Then there was just one song left.

'"Just Me"!' shouted Devi. And then they were all at it. '"JUST ME"! "JUST ME"!'

And I raised my eyes and looked into the audience to see that . . .

Adrian and Mands had gone from the front row.

Walked out.

Abandoned me.

Mum was looking at her feet.

And Lacey still wasn't there.

It *was* just me.

And I thought, some things you just can't forgive.

And they shouldn't forgive me. Because I'd been stupid to show off like this. Stupid to think that getting up in front of everyone would help.

My guitar began to slip from my arms.

''Scuse me.' It was Adrian, emerging from the stockroom with an armful of drum kit.

 331

Mands was clambering on to the teeny bit of stage that was left, slinging on one of Adrian's bass guitars. Jaz was coming up past me, drumsticks in her hands and now – now it was just like my bedroom – only, without . . . without . . .

It was at that moment that we all heard this rumble, far away at first, then gathering into a roar. Outside the people jumped apart, as something . . . someone . . . came hurtling through the crowd, scattering phones this way and that.

And then I saw what it was . . . and it was like . . . it was like . . . it *wasn't* like anything I have ever seen or heard or imagined.

It was Lacey, being carried along above the mass of bodies, half surfing, half flying, while something – some-one – charged through, ramming a path to the door.

Finally, as they broke through to the front, I saw.

Bleeding from a scratch above the eye, hair crazy, eyes basically feral . . .

Lacey was riding Nicole.

And it was *magnificent*.

Adrian was holding a tambourine.

And as Lacey reached out her hand, I knew it was going to be all right.

CHAPTER THIRTY-FOUR

'Yikes,' said Lacey, staring down at her phone. 'Have you seen this? You have to see this.'

COX IN CONCERT

She shot to fame with her homemade video of the gloriously cheeky 'Just Me', then vanished from view. But last night Katie Cox made a return to our computer screens with an intimate, live-streamed, one-off concert.

Cox seemed nervous at first, her hands visibly shaking. But after a few stumbles, she got into her stride with a set so electrifying, so well-crafted and so heartfelt that the early jitters were quickly forgotten.

Explaining the recent disappearance of the video that made her name, Cox said that she'd recorded 'Just Me' as a single with the uber-label Top Music (home to the likes of Karamel and Crystal Skye) but that her track had inexplicably been held from release.

Indeed, it was the teen anthem 'Just Me' that finished the set, with the backing of the same rag-tag group that had featured on that bedroom recording. Was it as good as the video watched by two million people?

No. If they'd rehearsed even once since making the original, then it didn't show. Endearingly, this did not seem to matter to Cox, whose smile lit up the room even as her song was abandoned before the second verse.

And perhaps it's that smile that so appeals to her fans. A number of different recordings of the concert exist, of varying quality, but a rough tally of their views thus far shows that from an initial audience of a few hundred, the show has already been downloaded more than 900,000 times.

Amid a frenzy of press interest, CEO of Top Music Tony Topper vehemently denied that the single 'Just Me' had been shelved, saying, 'There must have been some kind of miscommunication. I adore Katie. We had a terrific time in the studio and she's back in soon to talk about her album. We couldn't be more excited.'

So basically, it was the next day and we were at school, sitting around the back of the labs, sharing out a bar of chocolate that Jaz said she'd pinched from Aldi. Only, I found a receipt in the bottom of the bag, so, you know. Jaz says she's an anarchist who doesn't live by the rules, but someone paid for that Green and Black's with exact change.

'The best bit was when that girl got arrested for trying to kick the door down,' said Jaz.

'The best bit was when you said nice stuff about me,' said Lacey.

They were both good, although I have to say the girl trying to whack through the back door with steel toe-capped boots while screaming my name was a little worrying until the police got it sorted.

Anyway, though, they were wrong. The best bit was when I was putting my guitar away and I saw Adrian slip his arm around Mum's waist and she didn't shrug him off or anything.

There were loads of great bits that night, and I hope it doesn't sound like showing off or anything, but I do want to say them because they are important.

The first was that I barely saw Amanda for the rest

 335

of the evening because they kept the shop open after I'd finished, and everyone was asking her where they could get my songs, which obviously they couldn't. Only, Mands didn't let that worry her in the slightest and was getting people to sign up for her mailing list and promising another concert at the same time next week and recommending albums here, there and everywhere, and best of all, people were actually buying them. I even heard one guy saying that he was pleased that Harltree had finally opened up a music shop because he'd been waiting long enough.

All while Amanda was rushing around in this happy blur, Mum and Adrian were off talking in the stockroom, and when I put my head around the door to see about maybe going to McDonald's or something, I found them kissing. I screamed, obviously, and said it was the most disgusting thing I'd ever seen, to which Mum gave me the finger. While still mid lip-lock.

Mum rocks.

After all that, the rest of the night was a bit of an anticlimax, to be honest, as we waited around for the street to empty out and Lacey remembered about the fringe cutting and got stuck in with her scissors.

Eventually it rained and everyone went off and we got in the car and drove home, where we found that a big new leak had appeared in the roof and part of the hall ceiling was now on the hall floor.

Weirdly, though, after all that craziness, and the fact that the house really did seem to be doing its best to fall down around our ears, I slept incredibly well that night. And even though I was woken up early by Adrian banging on my bedroom door, which meant he must have stayed over, I felt this amazing sense of peace.

'Katie, can you get up?' He leaned around the door. 'We need to have a chat about something. Everything. Up you get, Katie. I've put the kettle on.'

He had also put on Mum's flowery dressing gown, which was such a crime against humanity that I said I would only come down if he got dressed. I did say it in a nice way, though.

Well, fairly nice.

Half an hour later and we were a reasonably OK-looking pair sitting at the kitchen table eating leftover Chinese takeaway, although not the rice, because as I told Adrian, you shouldn't eat leftover rice. Nicole once half heated up some egg-fried special and puked so hard that bits of her stomach came out and she had to go on a drip.

'Right. I—' He saw my hair. 'Oh God. I'd forgotten about that.'

'I know,' I said, feeling around on my forehead. 'It'll probably be OK once I've styled it. I hope.'

'You think?' said Adrian.

'No,' I admitted. 'But it was worth it to have Lacey back. Anyway, what's the drama?'

'I've had a message from Tony,' said Adrian. 'Quite a few, actually.'

Bear in mind that it was still eight thirty in the morning.

He held out his phone. 'Want to listen?'

'Not really,' I said.

'Sure?' said Adrian. When he saw that I wasn't going to take it, he carried on talking. 'He was calling to say that he was sorry if you and he had a bit of a misunderstanding in his office the other day . . .'

Which made me sit right up, I can tell you. 'There was nothing to misunderstand! He was *very* clear.'

'Well,' said Adrian, sticking his fork into a sweet and sour chicken ball that I'd had my eye on, 'Tony was very

 338

clear to me, too. Your single is out.'

My mouth went slack, so it's probably just as well I hadn't eaten it.

'*Out* out? As in, for people to buy?'

'Yup.'

'But . . . why?'

'Doesn't look good, big music man bullying a teenager. I don't think he had any choice. Especially not once Karamel came out in your support.'

'Karamel?' Savannah would *freak*.

'There's been a bit of interest in your concert, too. In fact, there's been a bit of interest altogether. Online petitions, people calling from the papers . . . You should probably take a look.'

'I'm going to have a break from the internet for a few days,' I told him, at which he nodded and said that was probably a good idea and he could see why I would want to but maybe not *these* few days.

Then the front door went and it was a delivery bloke with an enormous bunch of flowers. Not to sound ungrateful, because no one had ever sent me flowers before so it was really pretty excellent, but they looked a bit too big and exotic for our house. As if we'd pinched them from a hotel. There were handmade chocolate truffles, too (and I'm never going to be down on truffles), plus a card, which said:

To Katie

With love from all at Top Music

It was signed by a load of people I didn't know, and there, in the bottom corner, Tony. The nerve!

I almost admired him.

Almost.

'So what are you going to do?' said Lacey, who was attempting to make a daisy chain and, I have to say, failing.

'Well, I've got detention every night for the next week for skiving. Even though McAllister said she liked the concert. Can't have liked it that much, can she?'

'I meant about the music stuff,' said Lacey.

'Oh. That.' Somehow, I was finding it all a bit difficult to say. 'They want me to go back and talk about doing an album.'

'Cool.'

'Do you want to be on it, Lace?'

'Seriously?' said Lacey.

'Seriously,' I said, and I meant it too.

'Then, no, not really. Those music people sound horrible. But –' she gave my knee a squeeze – 'thanks for asking.'

'We're having this big fight with them because they are saying it has to be in school time and we're not going to take any days off.'

'You have the option to miss school and you're not even taking it? You are mad,' said Mad Jaz.

We all sat there for a while, and I heard the people talking in the dining hall and the seagulls that hang out on the playing field and some year sevens having a fight, and I felt, sort of, happy. Like I was in the right place, for a change. That the people I was with were the right people, and more than that, *I* was the right person. Which I hadn't experienced since the divorce. In fact, not for months and months.

'Give us a quid, babes,' said Savannah.

'No. Why?'

'I'm downloading your single, but I'm not paying for it.'

It would have been nice for her to have made this clear before she'd hit BUY, which I was about to tell her, when she gasped.

'What? Actually, don't tell me. I'm thinking I need a few days screen-free . . .'

'Number two.'

'Number two what?'

'"Just Me" is at number two.'

'You are literally making no sense right now.'

'You're at number two. In the iTunes chart. Between Karamel and Taylor Swift.'

'Show me.'

She did.

There was 'Just Me', with my name underneath in those neat grey letters, looking so incredibly proper. And there was a little picture of my face, a still from the video, with my mouth open.

Huh.

Was I ready? No. Not even slightly.

Was it what I wanted?

Not any more than I had to start with.

Probably, in some ways, quite a lot less.

There was only one way to deal with this.

'Lacey,' I said, 'can I come over to yours tonight? I quite want to watch *Mean Girls*.'

'*Mean Girls*! I'll be there,' said Jaz.

To which Lacey folded her arms and said, 'Er, I don't think so.'

'Please?' said Jaz.

'Why?' said Lacey.

Jaz looked away and said, 'You two seem like you have fun together.'

I thought: It must be pretty lonely being Jaz. Having to be mad all the time, when occasionally you just want to hang out and eat chips.

And then I thought how lucky I was to have Lacey back as my BFF, and I gave her a look that said, *Let's open up the arms of friendship to someone less fortunate than we are, even though she is a bit mental sometimes.*

'All right, you can come,' said Lacey.

Which must be the first time one of my faces has worked. Ever.

'But don't steal anything,' said Lacey. 'And don't record us on your phone and stick it online, and don't wind up my mum because I've already had my allowance

 343

suspended for the last two weeks in a row and there are things I need to buy.'

Jaz said she wouldn't.

Savannah flicked her hair.

Nicole was attempting to remove her cuticles with a vegetable peeler.

And I tried to imagine all those people listening to my song, and watching the concert, all those pairs of eyes in bedrooms and on buses and maybe sitting out behind the labs at their schools too, the millions of invisible connections between me and them, between my words and their ears, and for a second, just a second, I thought maybe I could.

And then the whole thing dissolved and it was just me, and Lacey, and Jaz and Nicole and Sofie and Savannah and Paige. And Amanda, over at the shop, sending out the first message to her new mailing list, and Mum and Adrian ringing the builders and probably doing something disgusting too.

I suppose I knew that things were about to change, but in my head, just for that second, I pressed PAUSE on the moment, so I could enjoy it. Come back and live in it, sometimes, when things got difficult, which I knew they would. But having one moment where everything was in balance, maybe that would make it OK.

And then I thought: Wow.

That's a great idea for a song.

ABOUT THE AUTHOR

Marianne Levy spent her twenties as an actor. She was in various TV shows, did some comedy on Radio 4 and made a brief appearance in the film *Ali G Indahouse*, where she managed to forget both her lines. She then worked as a continuity announcer for Living TV, introducing, and getting obsessed with, *America's Next Top Model*. She's been the voice of a leading brand of make-up, a shopping centre and a yogurt. Marianne has written for the *Independent*, the *Independent on Sunday*, *How to Spend It*, the *Guardian* and the *i*. She lives in London with her husband, daughter and a bad-tempered cat.

www.mariannelevy.com

Katie Cox's story continues in . . .

I WAS ABOUT TO SING LIVE TO TWELVE AND A HALF THOUSAND PEOPLE. AND EACH AND EVERY ONE OF THEM WANTED TO KILL ME.

Katie Cox (overnight singing sensation and owner of the World's Wonkiest Fringe) never meant to become a pop star. And she didn't mean to start a war with Karamel (aka the World's Cheesiest Boy Band).

Now her first concert is just days away. Cool? Maybe. Terrifying? Definitely. And with her friends more interested in her fame than her feelings, and an army of Karamel fans ready to take her down, this battle goes way beyond the charts . . .

OUT NOW!